About the Author

Ogonna Juliet Nnamani (nee Okpalaugo) is a Nigerian-Swede currently residing in Sweden. She is a wife and a mother of three who enjoys reading and writing. Her deepest emotions are expressed in poems and stories. She is discovering the dynamics of humans and the beauty of life as she relates with people from different walks of life. She is also a crypto enthusiast and a member of the Crypto Elites Club.

Choices

Ogonna Juliet Nnamani

Choices

Olympia Publishers
London

www.olympiapublishers.com
OLYMPIA PAPERBACK EDITION

A CIP catalogue record for this title is
available from the British Library.

ISBN: 978-1-80074-385-4

This is a work of fiction.
Names, characters, places and incidents originate from the writer's
imagination. Any resemblance to actual persons, living or dead, is
purely coincidental.

First Published in 2022

Olympia Publishers
Tallis House
2 Tallis Street
London
EC4Y 0AB
Printed in Great Britain

Dedication

To my family…

Acknowledgements

Thank you to my husband, Chris, for his support and to my children for their understanding. A special thanks to Fr Mike Akpan for his support and to Dr Chinwendu Okoro for explaining the medical terms used in the book. To Anderline Ibe, thank you for encouraging me to write this book and Dr Stella Orim, thanks for reviewing it. God bless you all.

Chapter 1

It was sometime after mid-summer, or so it was believed. She never really understood the seasons, although she had only been there for a year. She learned the months of the seasons online but the weather seemed to write its own script. Moreover, no one ever explained to her why Sweden celebrated their mid-summer in June, or maybe she never asked. The month of May was frigid, and it even snowed a couple of times! So how could June be the middle of summer? She doesn't understand the system anyway and couldn't care less about the weather at the moment as long as it was friendly enough for a walk. Her thoughts were doing a marathon. She didn't know what to believe or even what to think. Her mind was barred by the realities she discovered.

They were supposed to be perfect, next to God and living in ideals!

Life wasn't as smooth as she had thought it would be. She had an ideology, she believed in some principles, they should know better, live better, and relate better. She thought she had a clear path. She thought she had gotten to her destination. It turned out she hadn't. She was named Uzoma, which literally meant a beautiful path. Her parents wished that she would tread on a smooth path throughout her life's journey. Not that these wishes ever meant anything to her. In fact, she never spared her name a thought and much less now, when her beliefs seemed to be crumbling. How much she really didn't know. She felt so empty. Oh, this hollow she felt inside, when did it all begin?

Lost in thoughts, she waddled. It was a little windy. Her flowy black gown swayed like it had no care. For a while now, she had taken to black because of her depressive moods. It was her third day walking her afternoons away in this park, her thoughts rambling on nothing in particular. Then suddenly she was jolted by hands on her shoulder. Uzoma turned, wondering who had touched her.

"What the hell do you think you're doing?" she snapped. "You…" Her tongue trailed as she looked him up critically. "… White mule. What are you now? A good Samaritan? How dare you lay your filthy hands on me?"

The man simply stared with his mouth agape, dazed.

"Oh, what now?" she continued. "The cat has cut your tongue, or you simply have no vocabulary to wash your shame."

"I… I…" he stammered. He didn't know what was more embarrassing, the English language he had gained mastery of that chose to fail him at this conspicuous hour, his righteous deed gone awry, or this ungrateful loathsome lassie that rattled him.

"I thought as much. Nothing good ever came out of a blue-eyed wandering urchin like you." With one last glance at him, she stomped away.

Stefan remained on the spot wondering what just happened. All he wanted to do was steady her to prevent the mishap he judged was about to happen — a fall. He had thought to straighten her, but that brought out the fire in her.

"What just happened now?" he asked, turning to face his

12

date. He came to the park to enjoy the sunny weather with his… soon to be girlfriend, Stephanie.

"Maybe you should have minded your own business," Stephanie answered. Her eyes narrowed darkly with unspoken words.

At that moment, all Stefan wanted was to disappear. There were lots of people in the park that afternoon. Couples who had come to enjoy the sunny weather, children playing, and some teenagers sitting in groups. He scanned the people close by and noticed a few eyes on him. Some people did see what happened and that made him feel worse. There was no way he could sprawl out and pretend nothing happened. Finding his feet, he beckoned to Stephanie.

"Let's go, Steph. I can't stay here."

"Where do we go now?" Stephanie asked.

"Anywhere but here."

As they walked out hand in hand, Stefan still felt a little shaky. Holding Stephanie while they walked away, was his own way of staking his claims and silently communicating to onlookers that he had his own woman.

Nothing like this had ever happened to him. He's had it smooth and was adored by everybody. He had always been the most popular guy in school. All the girls wanted to be his friend. What was it she called him? A blue-eyed wandering urchin? He glanced at his covers. He was wearing a royal blue short-sleeved California top on brown shorts and well-fitting black loafers. He couldn't be looking bad. Besides, whoever gets offended with blue eyes anyway? All he's ever heard were praises for his blue eyes and blond hair. Not that he really cared about his hair and much less the color, but he'd felt proud a few times when he'd chanced upon descriptions of blond as ravishing beauty. Now this lady, whoever she was, flawed his preconceptions and self-esteem of what a perfect creation he thought he was. He was grateful for one thing: no one in the park seemed to have recognized him. At least he didn't hear anyone say anything. It was the most bizarre moment of his life.

He took Stephanie home. He was in no mood for outings any more.

As soon as he got home, he stepped into the shower, reliving all that happened earlier. He allowed the water to splatter as the words "wandering urchin" kept ringing in his head and the image of the girl haunted him. After several minutes of gazing into thin air, Stefan began to wash his face as though he could relieve it of this image that taunted it so. It had only been a couple of days since he returned from his unofficial round-the-globe adventure. His father had enabled him. As the owner of an international brand, Stefan's father, Erik, had the means to support his son. Besides, Stefan had worked for him full-time during summer and on weekends during school sessions for years and had a good sum starched. Erik understood his son's need to get away and see the world. He did too at that age. Erik had been to America, China, South Korea, and Japan. He had also been to many other European countries. It was on one of these trips that he met Stefan's mother, Alice.

Theirs had been an instant attraction. It was during a twelve-day cruise from Tokyo to Hong Kong. Erik met Alice at the outside deck, just by the stern, watching the departure, alone.

"Having a good time?" Erik said, more as a comment than a question. She had given him the most amazing smile he'd ever seen and sealed their fate from that moment. Alice, a German, had gone traveling, soul searching. She needed clarity on the route to take in navigating the course of her life. Meticulous as she was, she'd been known to steadfastly continue on any path she decided on till the end. Her major challenge had always been the hassle of choosing and the length of time she seemed to spend making decisions. For Alice, the trip provided alone time around nature for her reflection. She hadn't planned on any company, which was the reason she didn't travel with any of her friends.

At first, Erik had stolen a bit of her time the first day, then her thoughts. His charming face and carefree laughter were embedded in her soul and encroached on her musings. By the second day, she didn't want to be apart from him and by the third day, they had bonded as lovers. Stefan was conceived on that trip and they had gone official before God and their loved ones two years after.

Stefan had heard countless times tales of his parents' love. As a child, he was exasperated, even jealous of the attention and love they showered on each other. Sometimes, he felt like an intruder in their midst. He was their only child. With no siblings to turn to, he had relied on and spent most of his time with his friends, Peder and Anders. They lived in the same neighborhood, attended the same schools, and worked for Erik on weekends and holidays. Stefan loved his friends, but his utmost desire was to find his own version of his mother. He wanted what his parents had and more, only that he'd rather not have any child in-between his own love story, his silent competition with his father was the rationale behind his expedition. For six months, Stefan traveled to different continents and cities in search of his heartthrob. Like his father, he went on a cruise to different places and when he ran out of money — his savings through the years — he was forced to humble himself and ask his rival, his father, for assistance.

Neither time nor the places he visited, delivered Stefan his utmost desire. He had returned home in the middle of June, heart wrenched, feeling broken. Life became dreary and monotonous for him. He'd spent several days at home brooding before his friends convinced him on taking up a métier. He decided to work for his father again just to amass some funds, then take out a loan to build his own empire. He was still determined to outshine his father in any way possible. Stefan met Stephanie, a temporary employee in his father's establishment. She was beautiful, tall, and slender. A forest-green-eyed brunette with an appealing golden tanned skin. Stephanie's high cheekbones that accentuated her eyes, her straight nose and her small but sexy lips made her a striking beauty. Stefan was immediately taken by her looks upon their first meeting. His sexual forage had been nesting within and he didn't know. They might even fall in love! Stephanie laughed at his every joke and looked smitten. A romantic picnic by the park could seal their fate and blossom their love beyond what his parents shared. Their romantic picnic which was now destroyed by the stranger he only wanted to help.

Chapter 2

Four days in a row, Stefan staked out the park. He'd never been a quitter. Besides, the girl's image continued to assail him. Neither did her words cease to echo in his head. He knew everyone's opinion about him couldn't have been all savory, but no one dared to utter any impolite remarks in his presence. His peers treated him like a demigod for his perfect build, or so he thought, and for the rarest of things he possessed. Money plus looks placed him at the summit. Although he'd rather glory in the seat of his toils, his wealthy family provided much more than he was willing to give them credit for. Gifts from his parents and grandparents were not his supreme treasure. They were merely things money could buy and could hardly muzzle his desire. He hankered for all things money could not buy. Honor in his own name, not inherited, and a love greater than that of his parents.

He sipped his tea, glanced at his wristwatch and sighed.

"Dear Lord, draw that wisp to this garden today," he prayed. He was not an ardent believer in God, but his mother did instill some spirituality in him such that words like those often escaped his mouth when in dire need.

Stefan had given into fantasies of his victory over the lady he sought. His ultimate desire was to subdue her and get her to apologize or eat her words. He would succeed in this mission no matter what it took. He chose the coffee shop across the park for his hideout. It had a good overview of the park, so he would see her whenever she surfaced. He had a gut feeling that she would visit that park again no matter how long it took, and he was willing to dedicate time to his quest.

He sipped his coffee and checked his chats.

"Hey, can I have one cola please?"

The familiar voice arrested Stefan's thoughts. He looked up to find his hound right there in the shop. She must have passed when he bent down to respond to messages on his mobile phone. Stefan hurriedly covered his face with a book. What should he do? Should he approach her now or wait for her to get to the garden if she was headed there? He wouldn't want to be disgraced a second time.

"It's best I approach her as soon as she leaves the shop and before she gets to the garden," he whispered to himself.

He watched as she left the coffee shop and walked across the park. He simply watched! His legs couldn't move. It was unlike him to be intimidated by anyone, much less an immigrant. He swallowed hard and assured himself he wasn't scared of her, that he was only strategizing.

"I think I'll just wait and follow her, who knows what I'll discover," he thought.

He savored the idea.

"What if she's up to something? Or, maybe she's just a sadist. She could even be an illegal migrant." He smirked, then explored the idea further.

"If she is an illegal migrant, she'll be at my mercy. I will certainly make her chew her words! This is my country, my home, and taming this African would be the adventure of the century." He gave a wicked grin.

Uzoma sat by the lake in the park, lost in thought. She

needed to make up her mind: go back home or stay an extra year in this country. Her glee upon arrival a year ago had turned to glum. She was lonely. No family. No friends. All alone in this part of the world. Her mother's words a few days ago exasperated her.

"Ada, I do not want to hear such comments again and I hope you're joking about it.[1] How can you think of coming home without completing your education? What will people say? You are supposed to be the pride of the family, of the entire kindred, and even the country at large. Do you want to bring disgrace to the family? You know your cousins are jealous of you because of your smartness. Do you want them to laugh at us? You must finish your master's studies before visiting home. Afterwards, you can go back to obtain a doctorate degree. End of discussion!"

When she confided in her closest friend back at home, Ifeoma, her reaction was similar.

"Ada, try and loosen up a bit. We researched many countries before you chose Sweden, and that place from the pictures is a wonderful place. They are not racists and their policies are awesome. You even said so yourself. Ada, I think you're just lonely so I suggest you make friends. Loosen up. And what happened to your leap at love? Have you given up? Ada, please make the best use of the opportunity you have. I wish I were in your shoes."

No one seemed to understand her plight.

"They are not racists," she recalled Ifeoma's words and smiled. How can she blame her friend when she thought so

---

[1] Uzoma's family and friends called her Ada which means first daughter as an endearment.

herself and even preached it now she wasn't sure any more. She remembered the day she arrived. Her inexplicable feelings on the plane as she journeyed into the unknown were like a mixture of gall and vinegar. Excitement and anxiety churned her stomach so that she couldn't eat or drink anything. What would her life be like? Tears streamed down her cheeks. The reality had begun to set in. She was alone, completely alone! She looked to her right and left, her neighbors didn't seem friendly. She even tried to initiate small talk with the white guy on her right and received only monosyllables, a clear indication of his lack of interest. The woman on her left, a Nigerian, looked so stern and scary that Uzoma only offered greetings, bowing respectfully. Nigerians were big on respect. She'd simply buried her head in a book for the remaining part of the journey, feeling lonely. Maybe that was her clue about the days ahead, but she hoped anyway. The chilly breeze as she disembarked from the plane petrified her. She was in another 'world,' hours from home.

Her experience at the airport was thrilling. She had retrieved her luggage and, noticing the absence of security operatives, had lurched in search of them with her load.

"Can you please check my luggage so I can leave?" she said to the first security man she met.

"You can leave," he answered.

"How do you know I'm carrying my own bag if you don't check," Uzoma insisted.

"We know you'll take your own bag. And even if you mistakenly take another's, we know you'll return it," was the response she got.

Astonished, she picked up her phone to call her parents and friend.

"Now that's what I'm talking about. They recognize that we are humans and humans are trustworthy! I knew it, Mom, this is the best place for me. Not the UK," she boasted.

Uzoma's mom had wanted her to go to the UK so she would be close to her aunt and cousins, but Uzoma was adamant, not after reading the glamorous tales of Sweden. Besides, she knew her mother's real intent, to clip her wings, that is to limit her freedom, as culture demands.

"Our people frown at a young lady living alone. It will deprive her of suitors," Uzoma had overheard her mother say to her father. And that had also strengthened her resolve to go to Sweden.

"What an adult sees sitting, a child cannot see even when he climbs on the top of an iroko," her mother retorted as she lashed out at her for her insistence. Yet it seemed she made the right decision; she was finally in a perfect world and this first experience confirmed it.

Uzoma felt proud and victorious as she boastfully narrated her airport experience to her mom. She even added, "this time, Mom, you're wrong and I'm right. This is the twenty-first century. It's time you dropped that adage that indicates that adults knew better than the young."

Uzoma smiled dryly as she recollected all this. After some hours of brooding by the lake in the park, she made her way home. She lived a good distance from the garden yet she walked rather than taking a hurl. As she walked mindlessly, Stefan followed at a close distance, determined. After walking for almost forty minutes, Uzoma turned around. She suddenly had a gut feeling she was being followed. There, she saw him — the guy in the park from last time, trying to dodge behind a pole. She made her way towards him.

"You coward," she bellowed, "why are you following me? You malign hippopotamus." She almost broke down. No. She won't let herself cry before this enemy, not now, not ever!

She turned and climbed the little hill to her abode.

Again, she turned. This time, Stefan was only a few steps away from her.

"I hate you," she said, barely audible.

"What?" Stefan asked. He couldn't believe his ears

"I. Hate. You," she retorted. "I hate everything about you. Everything."

She opened the entrance to the building, walked in and slammed the door behind her. Stefan stood at that spot transfixed.

"How can she hate me when she doesn't even know me? Could it be a result of what happened in the park? I only wanted to help, to steady her. What could be so wrong with that? If anything, I deserve gratitude and not this attitude. And why does she look so forlorn?" He felt an overwhelming need to know.

Stefan retreated. He knew she would be back. He could investigate her, ask someone to investigate her. His friend, Peder, could help. They could come up with tricks that could foster his ploy. No, he wanted to wield this baton alone. If she had any skeletons, he'd rather find out himself and twist her arms properly before handing her over to the authorities. Not that he was a violent person, or that he would ever physically abuse a lady, but he would wring humility out of her. The nerve of her to humiliate him in his homeland! And what exactly impels someone to 'hate' another? He was certain he had never met this lady prior to the day at the park. If only he knew her name.

Chapter 3

"You again," Uzoma said softly.

"Wait. I understand that you don't want to see me and that you hate me, but I have just one question for you. Why do you hate me?"

Uzoma stared at him for a while, completely taken aback by his question. She was exhausted. It had been a busy day for her.

"Follow me," she commanded.

Stefan hesitated a little but did her bidding and followed her into her home. She lived in a one-bedroom apartment properly sectioned into a kitchen, a sitting area, and a sleeping area. A white transparent curtain was used to demarcate the sitting and sleeping area while the cooking area was at the left corner of the room with a door leading to the balcony.

"Do you care for anything? Tea? Coffee? Food? I have some Jollof rice. It's a little spicy but nice."

Stefan was confused. He couldn't imagine his enemy being hospitable. Would it be safe to accept anything from her?

"Water would be fine," he decided.

Uzoma gave him water, disappeared into the bathroom on the right for a couple of minutes and returned looking refreshed. She still had that forlorn look. She dished the Jollof rice for herself and sat down to eat.

Stefan just watched silently.

"So, why do you hate me, Augusta?" Stefan asked when she was done eating.

"How did you know my middle name?"

"I saw your name on the door. I'm not sure how to pronounce your first name so I opted for the middle. I don't know what my crime is, and I'd rather not compound it when I'm yet to assuage your disdain for me."

Uzoma smiled.

"My name is Uzoma. It's easy to pronounce."

"Uzoma," Stefan attempted, loving it.

"So, why do you hate me?"

Uzoma gazed at him for a while.

"I do not hate you. I hate what you represent," she said.

"And what is it that I represent?"

"Whites. You are white."

"And how is that a crime?"

Again, Uzoma stared at her guest silently for a couple of minutes, studying him. Now his blue eyes didn't irritate her any more, rather, they radiated calmness. He was wearing a white t-shirt that had a blue image of a ship on a river. He wore shorts, which was common for men in Sweden during summer.

"What's your name?" she asked. "You never introduced yourself."

"Stefan."

"Stefan, I am sorry I said those things to you. I'm usually not an arse, but from my experience in this kingdom, people treat me in three ways. Many don't care whether I burn or roast. Some act like they do when in reality they don't and the rest act like they pity me. Your action at the park shows you're either pretending or you pity me, none of which I need."

"When you say it like this, it sounds bad. Yes, you did

look pitiful, but I only tried to prevent you from falling and embarrassing yourself."

"And what makes you think you had the right to do that? Embarrass myself? What makes you think so? Why would I be embarrassed? I have been in worse situations, all right. You had no right to do that!"

"Hey, calm down. I'm just..."

"I think you should leave. Now," she said coldly.

Uzoma sank on the floor after Stefan's exit, feeling more depressed.

"Babe, I did it again. Maybe I'm really an arse," she said to Ifeoma on the phone and recounted all that transpired.

"The nerve of him to declare that I'd have embarrassed myself without him. Can you imagine that? He's just full of himself and you know I'm an antidote for puff daddies. If I wasn't in an awful mood already, I'd have deflected his ego."

"Calm down, Margaret Thatcher. I still don't understand why you're so angry. This is unlike you. Why are you so mean to this guy? Could it be that you find him so attractive that you're irked?" Ifeoma refuted.

"You're just a..."

"Shh. Tell me, what does he look like?"

"Do I know? A typical Swede."

"And what is this typical Swede look?"

"He's tall and slim, blond hair like anyari, and dreamy blue eyes.[2] He's definitely not my spec."

"Sounds like your dream man to me," Ifeoma pressed.

Uzoma ended the call. She was very close to saying something to her friend for which she would apologize for.

---

[2] albino

Ifeoma was her closest friend, even more like the sister she didn't have. For the love they shared, Uzoma's parents had stepped in to support her when necessary, to ensure that the girls attended the same schools always and had each other. The exorbitant fees of schooling in Sweden had been a hindrance to their tradition this time. They've been together for fourteen years. Ifeoma knew her friend and sister Uzoma harbored the desire of dating a white guy, a handsome, blue-eyed white guy with dark hair.

"Never in my fantasies did I imagine a blond, for crying out loud! And all those fantasies about white guys were before I knew better!" Uzoma declared to herself. Stefan was definitely not her type.

At home, Stefan got busy. A simple search on Google gave him some basics. Uzoma was a Nigerian student in Sweden, an International Relations Master's program student who arrived in Sweden only a year ago. The proper documentation of data in Sweden makes information easily accessible. Basic information about anybody can be found on the internet including home address, key dates, properties owned (such as cars and houses), annual income, etc. One of the pictures of Uzoma on the internet stunned her inquisitor. It was nothing like he had ever seen. He downloaded the picture and studied it for hours. Her dressing was unique, probably traditional. He wasn't sure but it was certainly not the kind of dressing he saw in the west. She was wearing two big waistbands with something that looked like a short skirt. Even the fabric was nothing like he'd ever seen. Her top was very short, a little above the navel, and had no sleeves. Her lower abdomen was gloriously exposed. Stefan swallowed hard, another part of him attentive too. Her neck was fully beaded with four beads of different lengths, designs, and sizes. Her hair was braided, packed in different balled shapes and beaded. She was barefoot and was wearing ankle beads as well. The look in her eyes held a promise, glittering. She was smiling. She looked so innocent and happy. Where did this girl go? What shrunk this beauty into the grim lass she had become? He resolved to find out.

Stefan printed the picture on paper. She had become his muse. He had seen her raw beauty while he watched her in her home earlier in the day. She had no makeup on and had packed her hair to the back. She had dark circles underneath her eyes, an indication of her unhappiness. She really did look pitiful, the one adjective she loathed and one that perturbed him.

"Wow, what a damsel. Is this our adversary? Damn, she's beautiful," Peder declared.

Peder referred to Uzoma as an adversary because he was privy to Stefan's discomposure.

Stefan, who was accustomed to spending time with Peder and Anders in the evenings, had gone solo. They were close friends, only months apart in age. Of the trio, Stefan was the tallest and slimmest. Anders had more body build, and a hoarse voice. He was austere. Peder, the shortest, was also the most affable. Peder and Anders knew Stefan was riled for days now. They also knew of the skirmish that unnerved him. It was the day Stefan was slated to go formal with his latest crush, Stephanie. He had gone out alone because he needed his privacy with Stephanie and had returned cursing his day and repeating the words of a strange lady. When Peder and Anders pried, he narrative the absurd events that marred his date with Stephanie. He had since then 'hunted' — as he would say — alone.

"Don't call her that," Stefan, who was lost in thoughts and

oblivious of Peder's entry, defended.

"Easy, raccoon," Peder bantered, "what has this girl done to you? Now, I understand why you're so riled. You're in a brawl with someone you'd rather… Wait a minute, is that admiration I see in your eyes?"

"Get out, Peder. Let me breathe. And purge your mind of those risqué thoughts. I know you."

"Hmm. Now I know why you won't let me tag along these days. So, what's the update on our chase?"

Stefan hesitated at first, but the need to confide in someone compelled him to divulge all he had discovered and experienced earlier. Peder noticed his dreamy eyes and the intensity with which he spoke and realized the depth of his avidity.

"Let's check Facebook or other social media platforms for more private information about her," Peder suggested.

They found her Facebook page. Her privacy settings obscured their exploration. Her profile picture was another stunning picture, a headshot of her in light makeup. Her cover photo was a beautiful top shot of an unknown location that had a pedestrian bridge, some tall modern buildings, and a good number of people, black people.

"Maybe this is somewhere in her country," Stefan said.

Although the picture didn't look anything like he would imagine of an African country, and the people in the picture didn't look like the hungry malnourished people in the adverts he had seen on television, there were no other deductions he could make from the picture.

Chapter 4

The next few days were tangential for Uzoma, who kept hoping Stefan would surface. She owed him an apology, again. She had deliberated within herself countlessly, justifying her actions and reprimanding herself for being so irascible. If only she could see him, she could simply apologize and maybe they could become friends. He could be her first Swedish friend. In her opinion, Swedes were not very friendly and would rather keep to themselves. Uzoma even went to the park a few times hoping to see him!

"Maybe he got tired of being berated," she thought to herself as she walked home from the park one evening.

"Well, good riddance."

After two weeks of waiting and yearning, Uzoma gave up. She had blamed herself enough and it was time to move on. Unfortunately, Stefan could have been a friend. She even imagined it. The few non-black men that indicated an interest in her in the last year only wanted her body. She could easily tell from their lustful looks, sizing her up. She had curves in the right places, appealing boobs a little bigger than a handful, a flat tummy, nice curvy hips, and full legs. She was slim by Nigerian standards, but she was plumper than most girls in her class. Her femininity was the asset that made men drool over her, only goons irritated her, like the one that once approached her in a second-hand shop. She had fitted a spring denim jacket she wanted to buy and was appreciating its suitability when a white-looking man approached her. Prior to her time in Sweden, Uzoma thought humans were simply either blacks or whites. She only learned after she came to Sweden that there were categories of whites and that not all fair-colored non-Africans could fit into the description of 'whites.' The man sized her up severally before telling her she was beautiful. The hunger in his eyes could not be missed.

"How long have you been in Sweden," he asked Uzoma

"Less than a year."

"Do you have a resident permit?"

"Yes. Why do you ask?"

"If you don't have, I could help," the man offered.

"Thanks, but I do have a resident permit."

"Do you have a boyfriend?"

"Yes, I do." Uzoma lied. "If you'll excuse me, do have a nice day."

Disheartened that day, Uzoma had walked home imagining what could have happened if she wasn't a legal migrant. That man would have treated her no less than a whore all in the name of assistance. A man who spared no time for her face and was rather fixated on her body even during the interaction. She knew she had a body that could sway men, but she wanted a man that would be attracted to her for her intellectual capabilities. A man that would love her and laugh at her dry jokes. A man that would see her first before her body. Such a man would love her even when her body withered just like her father, Amechi, loved her mother, a love that kept their family together.

As Uzoma was an only child, a female, her father, Amechi, was pressured by his family to marry a second wife or get a concubine to bear him a son. Male children were very significant in her tribe. They inherited properties, not females. They attended the kindred meetings and carried on family legacies.

"Your daughter will marry and leave this house. Who will inherit your wealth? Who will carry on your name?" her paternal grandmother had said to her father one day.

"I love my wife and will not remarry. My younger brother has a son who can carry on the family name," was her father's reply.

Uzoma was proud of her father not because she was certain her father would not keep another family, he could be hiding another family, but because he loved her mother enough to defend her even before his own family. He could be truly smitten by her mother's beauty, a beauty true to her name, Mmachi, meaning God's beauty or beauty from God.

Sometimes Uzoma would imagine another woman barging into their house to declare that her father was the father of her children, boys. It could happen, she had heard of many such stories. Ekenem's dad, Mr Onyema, who owned one of the finest houses in the estate they lived on, did that and Ekenem was a male child, the only male child out of four children by his mother Azuka. Aunty Azuka, as Uzoma called her as a sign of respect for an older person, was her mother's friend who had taken recourse in their home crying on her mother's shoulders for days. A bleach-skinned woman with heavy makeup had appeared at Mr Onyema's house one morning with two boys claiming that Mr Onyema was the father of her children. Azuka had called the lady a gold digger, a tramp, and a liar. She had willed her husband to deny the allegations and throw the woman out of their house. Rather,

her husband had admitted that the children were his. According to Mr Onyema, Azuka only gave him one son, which was risky.

"A one-eyed man lives in fear of losing his only eye," he justified. "Ekenem is still the first son and will inherit a good portion of my wealth."

"He betrayed me," Azuka cried on Mmachi's shoulders. "I gave him four lovely children. I almost lost my life the last time. My daughters are so beautiful and smart. I have been a good wife! I sacrificed my career, gave up on my dreams, and this is how he rewards me."

Uzoma could remember the despair in her mother's eyes as she cried with her friend. She knew her mom was thinking mostly about her own plight rather than the immediate pain her friend was going through. If Mr Onyema could do this to his wife for having one son, what would her own fate be with only one child, one daughter, and no son at all?

Uzoma's father did all he could to reassure Uzoma and her mother that he was faithful to them and had no secret family. For months, he tried to make his wife happy again. He showered gifts on Mmachi, got her a new car, a shopping plaza in her name, and gave in to Uzoma's desire to go to school in Sweden. Mmachi was vocal about her fears and even suggested adopting two boys, but Amechi would not have it.

"You and Ada are enough for me. I am a fulfilled and complete man. I need no son to validate me," her father had insisted. His words brought equanimity to his family, though their doubts were not totally dissipated. For Uzoma, the events fueled her desire to marry a white man who will not betray her over the issue of a male child. She had been quite hopeful at first when she arrived in Sweden, but the individualistic nature she observed in Swedes and what she felt was an unwillingness to mingle had dwindled that hope significantly. She was no longer certain she would find a white friend in Sweden and much less a lover.

Chapter 5

Stefan got to work the next day after his last adventure with Uzoma. His favorite department was the factory because of the smell of wood that stimulates his scintillating wit and the glorious feeling that accompanied his creative works. Theirs was a furniture industry. One natural resource in abundance in Sweden was good timbre and Erik knew how to convert this to good use. After his trip, Stefan's father, Erik, asked him to work in the administrative unit so that he could familiarize himself with the managerial aspect of the business. He wasn't particularly fond of office duties nor sitting in front of a computer all day. Stefan only accepted the offer because he felt he'd need the lesson for his own pursuit when he eventually got around to it. Stephanie's presence at the office was his only delight. That morning, Stephanie had gone to deliver some designs to him. Her combined scent of rose, lavender, and strawberry filled the room, permeating Stefan's gloom.

"How are you today?" Stephanie spoke softly to him, noticing his glum. She went over and nudged him gently then hugged him, a gesture that turned into a kiss and a warm caress. She ran her fingers down his spine as her mouth devoured his. He shoved her on the desk while his hands found her buttons. It took every ounce of restraint in him to propel her into convenience before giving in to their wild passion. It was something about the soothing voice of Stephanie, and the softness of her palms that got Stefan feeding off her platter in no time. She was radiating that morning; her scent and gentle whispers drove Stefan to the spot where she wanted him. A moment of madness, spontaneity, and adrenaline rush that made office romance thrilling. Maybe it was for the best, they had a connection that could be the foundation of Stefan's aspiration. The deed was done, he'd give their relationship a chance. Fate seemed in sync with his friend's ideology. Anders had spoken to him earnestly after Peder brought him to speed on Stefan's phantasmic romance with the unknown lady. Anders had always been the most rational of the trio.

"What exactly do you intend to achieve?" he had asked Stefan.

"She acted poorly towards you. Be the man, suck it up, and move on. Or are you falling in love like Peder claims? If you're not, I don't see the reason for your continuous invasion of her privacy. Let her be. She has made it known to you in more ways than one that she takes no delight in you nor your kind. I'll take a chance on Stephanie if you're not game."

Stefan beamed as he recalled his friend's words. Who knew the reserved-looking, delectable Steph had this streak of spontaneity to her? One could easily mistake her for a recluse, but surprisingly, she was bold, decisive, and dynamic. She had her arsenals, her protective gear ready as though she knew the morning coitus would happen, or she could be used to such extempore having exhibited such boldness and preparedness. Whatever it was, Stefan was grateful as the magic helped him cope with his decision to let Uzoma be. Besides, he couldn't turn back on Steph now, not after the deed that morning. It all seemed too logical so he leaned on to reason.

Over the next couple of days, their relationship blossomed with fine wine, cigarettes, and good sex. Stefan tucked the picture of Uzoma away hidden in between the books on his shelf. He would do his best to forget her. After all, she hated him and his like. Rather, he gave in to the full wit of his new girl. Some Fika breaks ended with a knock up in the bathroom, Friday nights clubbing were crowned with sex in the car, all on a high horizon that left Stefan catching his breath. He could hardly keep up. At first, it was fun. Then he tried to please her.

"I think we should end things," Steph said suddenly. "I mean it's been fun and I really like you, but I'm tired of pushing you. I practically drag you to do everything. This is not how I envisaged things or my life. I'm too young for this. I think I have to move on. We're not strangers though," Stephanie aired, not mincing words. Her ability to hit the nail without meandering was one of the characteristics Stefan loved about her. As reticent as she looked, she wasn't one to bottle up things. She wasn't the loud type either. She would never create a scene to get the desired attention. Rather, she was unapologetically blunt in a low pitch that sometimes contrasted the weight of her words.

"I understand," Stefan replied and hugged her. "I'm sorry you feel that way, but I did give us my best."

Stefan felt the hollow in his heart deepen with the breakup. He moved back to the factory to work. He needed the smell of the woods for his sanity. He wasn't head over heels in love with Stephanie, yet they had a connection, a bond, and most of all, she kept him moving rather than brooding. Sadly, he was back to the start and nowhere close to achieving his dreams or beating his father in the love game. Maybe love wasn't really for everybody. He did his best. He went on the love trip in search of his heartthrob. His past relationships didn't give him the gut feeling his mother described.

"When you see the one, you'll know," she had said. Would he really know? Sometimes he felt he must have missed 'the one.' She could be one of those he hadn't spoken to in a cafe, or on a bus, or a train. He wished things would be simpler or that someone could just point her out. He was craving for a love different from what his friends offered. The closeness between his parents only served as a reminder of what he didn't — couldn't — have. He started to sleep out, better to spend time with his friends than to be the third wheel in his home. Anders and Peder shared an apartment. They had moved out of their parents' homes after high school. Stefan crashed with them sometimes. He wasn't ready to leave his parents' home. He was waiting for love, for his partner. They would choose an apartment together and decorate it to their taste. Now, all he could do to cope with the hollow in his heart was crashing with his friends, his hope of finding true love ebbing away further.

On Saturday afternoon in the third week of September, tired of playing video games with his friends, Stefan strolled to the park. The weather was bright and cold and a little windy — typical autumn weather. The sun was up more for the light than the feel. It was fine weather for a walk, a break in a long week of rain. He would be damned if he didn't utilize it to unclog his brain. As he walked to the park, thoughts of Uzoma filled his head. He recalled their first encounter and smiled. If only he could see her again. Anders was right, he couldn't continue to barge in on her or he would be a stalker. He sprawled out in the park cherishing the memories of the feisty enchantress that stole his peace. He picked out his phone to drool over her picture on Facebook.

"There must be a way," he said to himself, feeling intense sadness and longing. He needed the right reason to show up at her doorstep or else bear the brunt if she decides to alert the police. Besides, her fiery self could very well burn him with words that could rob him of sleep for nights unending. "It might be better to see her and be tongue-lashed for it than this lost feeling," he considered. "Who knows, I could convince her to be my friend. I could be a listening partner, someone she could heap all that anger on, someone she can complain to about my race. But what exactly happened to cause her such grief and hatred? Who knows? I could help." Stefan lightened up, suddenly feeling like a hero. He would go to her if he could come up with a tangible excuse.

He stood up feeling happier. He decided to go to her place, he would come up with something concrete on his way. Hearty, he turned to sprint and there she was gazing at him.

"Hi, Stefan," she said. "We meet again."

Chapter 6

All her life, Uzoma had only dated one person: Ugochukwu, her long-time crush. They lived on the same estate and attended the same schools. Although Ugochukwu was her senior in school, Uzoma had been very fond of him and endeavored to get his attention at every opportunity. They hailed from the same tribe, the same state, the same local government area, but different autonomous communities. It would be so easy for them to marry, her parents would accept their union. Their communities were only a few miles apart. Uzoma nursed those feelings because she knew her parents would oppose her marriage to men from other tribes. Even those from the same tribe but from different states won't be easily accepted either. Ugochukwu was perfect in every sense. He was tall, smart, and handsome, very handsome. His family belonged to the upper class so he had it all. Uzoma did him favors. She'd hold his belongings when he played football, run errands for him when he demanded it, and lie to his parents when he needed a decoy. Their parents were at ease with their friendship.

"He is from a good family," Mmachi advised her daughter, "it will be great to have them as in-laws, but keep your legs shut. I don't want an unwanted pregnancy in this house." Mmachi and Ugochukwu's mother addressed themselves as in-laws in a frisky manner, prepensely wedging the idea into their picknies.

On many occasions, Uzoma had seen Ugochukwu with different girls, even played the role of a sister when he needed to please any of the girls. She hoped that Ugochukwu would come to love her and appreciate her kindness. They were friends at first, just friends until Ifeoma came up with the idea that made them more than friends. Apparently, Ugochukwu liked Uzoma but his pride made him keep her at bay. Spiking up the jealousy streak seemed the best game plan. They were all in the university at the time, the University of Lagos, not just because it was close to their homes but because of the prestige that came with being an Akokite.[3] Ugochukwu chose the University of Lagos because of the prestige and honor that came with it, Uzoma chose the school to be close to her crush and because it made her mom happy since the school was close to their home and her mom could see her at will, while Ifeoma tagged along for the sake of her friend-turned-sister, Uzoma.

Ifeoma had simply gotten one of her friends and coursemates, Edet, to act interested in Uzoma to spike jealousy in Ugochukwu. At first, Ugochukwu was all protective of Uzoma, warning her off Edet. He did his best to discredit Edet before Uzoma, which thrilled her. He caved in eventually in a prideful manner.

"You know our mothers want us to get married, I mean they even address themselves as in-laws as though we are married already. I don't want my future wife messing around with anybody," Ugochukwu commanded.

"You can't go around dating people and expect me not to

---

[3] students of the University of Lagos were called Akokities because the school was located in Akoka

do the same. Besides, our mothers might call themselves in-laws, but you've never asked me out," Uzoma said firmly. She needed him to commit to a relationship.

"Fine, be my girlfriend," Ugochukwu caved in.

Uzoma had thought happily ever after awaited them, that her fantasies had been birthed and life had become a smooth journey. Ugochukwu took her on dates to expensive places and showered her with gifts, expensive ones, especially when he felt guilty over something, mostly when he cheated. Uzoma had noticed traces of other women in his room, hair accessories that weren't hers, broken acrylic nails, and lingerie. Ugochukwu had blamed it on his friends, claiming they used his room in his absence and bought Uzoma gifts to make peace until she caught him in the act.

"It's all your fault," he said, "you won't allow me to touch you. You claimed you're keeping your virginity for your husband when we know we are going to get married eventually. I do my duties as a man, I buy you things, you should do yours as a woman and all these will stop."

Uzoma was heartbroken. She didn't know what hurt her the most, Ugochukwu's iniquitous acts or his proud defense. Uzoma knew men from her tribe were known for their pride. They were known to shower women with gifts because of their pride, but she didn't expect him to cheat. Uzoma wept bitterly. Ugochukwu's cheating was not the only thing that rocked their relationship. He had treated her as though he was her lord. He got offended whenever she missed his calls or when she tried to stand up to him. There was no room to challenge him, he wouldn't have it. The ordeal instigated her fantasies to marry a white man, not because a white man wouldn't cheat on her, but because she felt their ego and pride wouldn't be as large as those of her tribal men. She began to make deliberate efforts to deflate the ego of any man arrogant enough to flaunt it, hence an antidote for puff daddies.

The hurt Uzoma felt each time she recalled her failed relationship was dissipating. Rather, she felt silly for harboring feelings for such a hollow person. Still, she hadn't given up on love. She believed love was the essence of life, which informed her choices of romance novels and films. She loved Korean dramas because irrespective of the genre, the theme of love was always reflected. When she wasn't occupied with a movie or a book, Uzoma spent her free time fantasizing about a love story that could be. She had walked into the park uninspired and thought she might as well take solace in nature when she spotted Stefan. There could be a twist in her uneventful day. She approached him hoping to right her every wrong.

"Hi, Stefan. We meet again."

She wasn't certain what his reaction would be. If he reacted badly towards her, he would be the bad guy and she would be free from the guilt of the past weeks. She plunged into her undertaking hopeful, at least she happened upon him by chance, which was different from what he did when he stalked her.

Stefan was speechless. He was delighted to see her, but he was yet to frame his approach, so he trembled physically, and she smiled. She had such power over him and he couldn't comprehend why.

"How have you been?" she asked.

"Very well, thank you. And you?"

"I've been as good as I can."

Uzoma sprawled on the grass, willing Stefan to follow

suit. For a couple of minutes, they stole glances at each other, silently.

"What do you think of me? Be honest," Uzoma inquired.

Stefan deliberated silently. If he'd learned anything from his encounters with Uzoma, it was that circumspection was a necessity in dealing with her. He wouldn't want her running off before he could have a proper conversation with her.

"Are you scared? You're taking a lot of time to give me an answer. I don't bite, you know," Uzoma pushed. She observed his uneasiness from his facial expression. She gave him a smile to help him relax.

"I'm just not certain what to say or do when I'm around you because I can hardly predict your reaction."

"Fair enough," Uzoma replied, "I admit I've been quite edgy but don't worry, I won't torment you today." Uzoma had planned to apologize to Stefan whenever she saw him again, yet she found his discomfort around her amusing and chose to exploit it further. In her books, whites were supposed to be assertive, not whippy, especially in the face of inferior ones. After all, she didn't initiate the term 'white superiority.'

"Say something, Stefan. Are you usually this introverted or am I that intimidating?"

Stefan observed her a little more. "Well, I think you're beautiful and bitter about something. Why is color so important to you and what have whites done to you?"

"Do you not see color when you look at me?"

"No, I see a human being, a fellow human being."

Uzoma chuckled.

"I perceived you'd say this but it isn't true. We all see colors and pretending it doesn't exist won't make you any better than me or others. I'll tell you a story, nay, two stories that will prove to you that we all see colors.

"A friend of mine, Nneka, a Nigerian, took her seven-month-old daughter to an event grazed mostly by whites in Nigeria," Uzoma continued. "At the event, this lady discovered that her daughter was very hearty, in fact, the daughter laughed several times, especially when a white person spoke. People noticed and even joined the baby in the humor. The mother wondered at her infant. Nneka observed that when a black person spoke, the baby wouldn't laugh. She only laughed when whites spoke. She wasn't certain what to make out of this and if her analyses were not just figments of her imaginations. Some weeks later, when the baby was a month older, she took the baby to another event. The infant was in tears for some discomfort then suddenly started laughing when a white lady approached her mom to talk. This confirmed the mother's hypotheses."

"Okay. I still don't understand how this proves that we all see colors."

"Relax, Stefan, I haven't finished. The second story I have for you happened here in Sweden. I was in a shop one day with Aisha, a black lady living in this city, and her fifteen-month-old daughter, Crystabel, an adorable child. Crystabel roamed the shop gaily and when she saw some children, two white boys, she went after them to play. I observed that those children drew back and instead ran to their parents for protection. Crystabel still went after the boys, but the boys ducked behind their parents. Aisha went after her daughter and took her away.

Initially, I thought Crystabel was being a bully by giving the boys a chase, that the boys were probably introverted in nature until Aisha narrated why she changed Crystabel's preschool. According to Aisha, Crystabel was posted to a preschool in an area occupied mostly by natives due to a lack of space in the school she had applied for her daughter. During the two weeks of in-schooling in which she attended the preschool with Crystabel, as is the custom here, she noticed that other children withdrew from her daughter. Crystabel was the only black child in her class and other children gaped at her. If Crystabel touched any of the toys the other children were playing with, they would simply abandon the toy for her. Aisha said that this behavior was consistent for the two weeks she attended in-schooling with her daughter, so she had to request a transfer of her daughter to a school with more immigrants.

"Those children were innocent, but they could see colors. They simply reacted to the difference they were not acquainted with and that doesn't make them bad. I dare say I experienced something similar. When resumed my studies here, during the orientation week, I noticed that people avoided sitting close to me. When we were given a task, they'd work with me as with others but they won't sit near me. At some point, I decided to warm up to them myself," Uzoma smiled wistfully. "Regardless of my efforts, the only people that reciprocated and related with me were immigrants, Asians. Probably because they feel the same void I do. Others only communicated to me during group assignments. Again, Stefan, this doesn't make them bad. It might be a human phenomenon as I am beginning to understand, but, my dear, we all see colors, every one of us. We all notice the difference in others." Uzoma was proud of herself after she spoke. The first shock of strangeness she experienced in the foreign environment was beginning to give way to reason, that humans were probably alike in their relationship with strangers.

"Wow," Stefan offered, mostly for want of a better expression.

"Stefan, when we act like we don't see colors, it is not because we truly do not see colors in others, it is because we have chosen not to be affected by it, which could be good or bad. Some people are not affected by color and can relate with anyone irrespective of their skin color. Many of such people from what I've come to realize, were nurtured in a very diverse and multi-ethnic environment with people of different colors. Some people choose not to be affected by colors because they'd rather not confront the peculiarities they see in others. Such people simply avoid strangers with differences as much as they could. People are more comfortable with some level of normalcy, with what they are accustomed to. There are people who desire to relate with different others, as I was when I first got here. For such people, the primary experience can either fuel or quell this desire and hence affect their subsequent behaviors," Uzoma concluded.

Chapter 7

When Stefan returned home that day, he was in no mood for chatter with his friends. He had a lot to ponder. Maybe life wasn't really as straightforward as he thought. He'd never spared a thought for the things Uzoma brought to his attention. Which group did he belong to? He stepped into the shower, his favorite place for mental exercises. He epitomized all that Uzoma had said, he thought, reflecting deeply. Maybe he really did notice colors and maybe he'd been acting unaffected because he couldn't confront the peculiarities. Was that why he never mingled with people of color in his school days? He had mingled with immigrants before, but were they really of different colors? They were mostly Europeans.

Stefan remembered Absame, a Somalian guy in his class during his high school days. Absame approached Stefan at first because of classwork, then had asked to join Stefan and his friends for lunch.

"I accepted his offer. I wouldn't do that if I saw him differently," Stefan muttered to himself in the shower.

"But you and your friends felt odd hanging out with him," his alternate voice reminded him. Stefan sighed. He and his friends had felt very strange with Absame in their midst. It was a quiet lunch. Anders had fixed his headset, listening to music to make up for the lethargy. Stefan smiled wearily. He recalled their discussion afterwards. He and his friends had thought

Absame was a bit loud for initiating small talk and cracking dry jokes.

"Maybe we just aren't used to such jokes, it could be the reason his jokes weren't funny to us. We felt strange. He too must have felt strange being in our midst," Stefan mumbled. They thought he dressed weirdly, almost unkempt. Even so, Absame had some white friends, immigrants, a Bosnian and a Dutch guy. "That should count for something," Stefan mused. The Dutch guy could have been from a multicultural environment. After all, Amsterdam was known for its multi-ethnic diversity. Stefan snickered as the realization dawned on him that Uzoma could be right.

"Some people choose not to be affected by colors because they'd rather not confront the peculiarities they see in others," Uzoma's words echoed in his head.

"Maybe she's right, but I've never consciously made such decisions."

Stefan left the shower, draped his towel around his waist, and went in search of the image of the woman that stole his peace. He searched for the printed picture frantically on his bookshelf and sat perplexed, gazing at it. A knock on his door hauled him out of his cogitation.

"Hey, Stefan, will you... Your room is in a mess, what's with the books on the floor?" his father Eric asked.

"Papa, do you want something?"

"Stefan, I'd really appreciate it if you would come with me to Bologna to finalize the deal. I want that branch established before Christmas. And who is this... girl?" Erik asked, taking Uzoma's picture from his son.

"Tell me, Papa, what is the first thing that came to your mind when you looked at this picture?"

"She looks African judging by her dressing and her looks."

"You mean she's black?"

"Isn't that obvious? Who's she by the way?"

"Someone I know, a friend. I'd love to go to bed now, Papa. I'll consider your request." Stefan dismissed his father.

"We should chat sometime, we hardly do that any more these days," Erik added and left the room.

"Uzoma is right," Stefan declared, glaring at her picture again. "We all see colors indeed." Stefan lay down, recollecting the impulse that guided his hunt. Her color gave her away as an immigrant. He'd even felt she could be an illegal immigrant!

"How did I ever believe that I'm not affected by skin colors?" It seemed like his world was shaking. He'd sailed smoothly all through, hardly giving any thoughts to deep philosophies of life. Now, he realized there were so many things he probably didn't know, the world outside his world. Had he been jaunting through life nonchalantly? All he ever wanted was a love life stronger than that of his parents, and a booming business, a conglomerate, to build an empire with his lover and live life to the fullest. He wanted someone who was docile like his mother and yet a strong force driving him into his destiny. His mother, Alice, would never argue with his dad, at least not before him. It could be something relating to her spirituality, but she wielded a strong power and could get Erik to do her bidding. She spoke more with her eyes than her lips and had a frightening stare that could make one uncomfortable. Sometimes, Stefan wondered how his father could love someone so stern. He wished for a more vivacious person, someone who smiled often, bustling with life, someone who would creatively jolt him into new things. Stephanie filled the latter, but Stefan felt the absence of something, a void that she couldn't fill. He tucked the picture under his pillow, shut his eyes and drifted into a fretful sleep.

The next morning, Stefan decided to embark on the trip with his father. He needed time to figure out his friendship with Uzoma and also to learn the intricacies of the business which he hoped would come in handy in the future. During the journey, he was dingy and stared at Uzoma's picture, her words taunting him. She provoked thoughts in him, strange thoughts. He felt he hadn't lived right, he could have gotten to know Absame better, and all the others fate had tossed his way. He knew it wasn't his fault as he could deduce that much from her speech, but he felt guilty all the same. He should have done better, should have known better. As he stared at Uzoma's picture, he'd downloaded it from Facebook, he wondered what she'd say if she knew the impact of her words on him. He found himself blushing, reciprocating to the smiling image that kept him occupied.

Erik observed his son keenly. He recognized the girl in the picture, the same black girl from the previous day. He knew that look on his son's face. Stefan was obviously smitten by this girl, whoever she was.

"How are things with Stephanie? I noticed both of you were kicking off," he inquired. Erik had never interfered in his son's relationships, but he had an awkward feeling about this black girl.

"There's nothing between Stephanie and me," Stefan responded hoarsely.

"I thought both of you…"

"Ended things. There's nothing between us any more."

Stefan was getting agitated. His father was encroaching on his reflection. He missed Uzoma. Maybe he shouldn't have gone on this trip. He missed her smiles, the way she smirked when she was being sarcastic, her oblong face, her funny gestures. He missed her deeply.

"And who's the black girl again?"

"I told you, Papa, she's my friend."

"Be careful, I've heard stories. Sometimes all they want is just a resident permit or citizenship through us."

Stefan became exasperated. Why would anyone think that just because of her color?

"How can you say that? Do you know if she was born here or not? Do you know if she's a Swede or not? If she were light-skinned, would you have said so?"

"Calm down, I only meant you should be careful, that's all." Erik retreated.

Things became apparent to Stefan. He had judged his father a liberal person. He had people from different races as members of his staff. He didn't think a negative word about anyone could slip from his father, his mother maybe, but not his father. He was a jolly good fellow. Stefan was perplexed. How could he fault his dad when he himself had similar thoughts initially? He'd thought she could be an illegal immigrant. Would they have thought the same if she had light skin and blond hair? She was judged by her color, people's impression of her stemmed foremost from her color, which could explain her distress.

Renewed, Stefan decided he'd do his best to shield her from such torture as much as he could. He couldn't imagine living under scrutiny among people. He will shower her with love so that she would forget her misery. He would make

Sweden a home for her and absorb her pains. He was done considering. He'd love her to the moon and beyond. She deserves some happiness because she was human, an intelligent one at that. His love story would kick off, he'd show his father how it's done.

Chapter 8

"Hi, welcome," Uzoma greeted.

"The fiery queen welcomes me into her home, interesting."

"Don't be sarcastic, mister. Besides, I consider you my friend now." Uzoma winked at Stefan.

"Anyway, you're right on time," she added.

"For what?"

"I planned to cook before you got here, but since you're here, we'll cook together. Don't give me that look, I told you we're friends now, so I won't treat you like a stranger."

Stefan smiled heartily. He was glad he sent her a letter while leaving for Bologna. He'd written that he would come to visit her on Saturday. He should have gotten her contact number from her when they met at the park, but he'd been clasped by her deep philosophies and had forgotten. Thankfully, he knew her address and PostNord could be prompt with letter deliveries so he opted for their services. He'd woken up quite early on Saturday, jittery, wondering how receptive she would be. Despite her amiable disposition the last time they met, Stefan wasn't certain what her demeanor would be. He'd considered that she could have experienced something in the past few days that could make her resentful towards him. He restrained himself from going to her early in the morning. He got to her house at noon believing it was a good time to visit a friend.

Uzoma washed the rice and set it on fire. She gave Stefan two bulbs of onion to cut and made fun of him as he reacted to the sulfenic acid. Stefan laughed too. Next, she gave him some vegetables to cut.

"What exactly are we cooking?" Stefan inquired.

"Something that will steal your heart," Uzoma teased. "There's a saying in my place that the way to a man's heart is through his stomach."

"Do you really want to steal my heart?"

Uzoma gaped, she'd been careless with her words. She only meant to tease him but he'd taken it literally. She admired him. Suddenly his blue eyes felt seductive and a burning desire to taste his pink lips erupted within her. His hair was parted on the left and brushed to the right. Standing close to him, Uzoma realized he towered above her. She barely made it to his chest with her 169cm length. The thing about Swedes and heights, although she had seen a good number of short ones, this particular one standing right next to her fit their giant description.

"Tell me about yourself," Stefan requested.

"There's very little to know about me. You already know my name. I'm the only child of my parents. I come from the eastern part of Nigeria, but I was raised in Lagos, which is in the west."

Uzoma showed him pictures of her parents and told him of her best friend and sister, Ifeoma. Standing close to him as they looked at her pictures together made Uzoma tense and hot. When his hand brushed hers, she felt it, butterflies in her stomach! She had heard about butterfly feelings but had never felt it herself, not even with Ugochukwu. Something was wrong, she was falling in… lust she decided, it had to be lust. It couldn't be love. It must be his slim body and cute face or the gentleness with which he addressed her. Gazing at him, she undressed him in her mind.

"We better continue with the cooking," she said, pulling away from him. His countenance dropped as she pulled away. He was enjoying the intimacy. He tucked his feelings away and focused on his chore, slicing the vegetables — carrots, green beans, onion leaf, as she instructed.

"And here is your delectable fried rice, Nigerian version," Uzoma swanked when they finished with the cooking. She dished hers and invited him to do the same. She sprawled out on the floor in her sitting area. Stefan was confused. He didn't know whether to join her on the floor or eat on the table as he was accustomed to. He hesitated.

"Come, sit beside me. There's something about sitting on the floor while eating I bet you've never experienced."

"So is this a typical Nigerian food," Stefan asked as he joined her on the floor.

"How little you know about my country," Uzoma replied. "I wonder if there's anything like typical Nigerian food. For us, rice is an intercontinental dish. Nigeria is like Europe, I do not mean in population, I mean in diversity. The way you have Swedes, Italians, Germans, and the rest with different languages, different foods, music, and culture, that's how Nigeria is. We have many ethnic groups, with different languages, not dialects, distinct languages, foods, and cultures. My tribe is Igbo and my local dishes are totally different from that of the Yorubas or the Hausas, for instance. When I say totally different, I mean every word of it, distinct. Don't worry, I'll make something traditional for you sometime."

Stefan marveled silently.

"Do you mind? we could watch a Nigerian movie on Netflix? We can watch The Wedding Party, it's about a marriage between two people from two ethnic groups in Nigeria. That would give you an idea," Uzoma offered.

"Sure," Stefan accepted, thrilled.

They spent the day watching movies while Uzoma explained some intricacies and uniqueness of her people. Stefan was surprised by the Nigerian landscape and the people as he watched. He'd seen pictures and videos of hungry Africans and the constant adverts to feed African children or to provide clean water for them.

"I thought Africa reeked of poverty," he said, barely audibly. He didn't want Uzoma to react. Uzoma laughed, loud and hearty.

"First, my dear friend, Africa is a continent, not a country. So saying Africa is poor is like saying Europe is rich when some countries in Europe are not rich. Secondly, if I say this, you'll think I'm boasting but the truth is that Africa is the richest continent in the world. Hold on, before you say anything, let me explain. Africa has the largest concentration of natural resources in the world. From gold to diamonds to different mineral resources, you'll be amazed. For example, ninety percent of cobalt used to power phone batteries, laptops, even electric cars, are gotten from Africa and mostly from Congo. People dig up natural resources, gold, coal from their backyards. Yet some of these countries are suffering. Congo, for instance, despite being the highest exporter of cobalt and the very high demand for this resource, is still poor. Why? Find out for yourself, and find out the true meaning of poverty. Whatever you think, never believe anyone that tells you

Nigeria is poor, because it is richer than most countries. And yes, we have a good number of poor people too, no thanks to bad governance."

Stefan was speechless, he realized how little he knew about the world of the blacks, it seemed like a different world to him, and watching them on the television was very fascinating.

At the end of the third movie, Stefan was glad he came. He was thankful he met Uzoma too and really wanted to explore this friendship.

Ifeoma FaceTimed with Uzoma while Stefan tarried.

"Na, the anyari be that," she asked in pidgin English to code her words from Stefan. Uzoma moved closer to Stefan so that Ifeoma could get a clearer view.

"This one gallant shaa oo," Ifeoma exclaimed before making an acquaintance of Stefan.

"So, you like Ada?" Ifeoma inquired.

"Babe, kilode? Why you go de ask am that kind question?" Uzoma responded in pidgin, embarrassed.

"You mean Uzoma?" Stefan asked, confused. He couldn't quite grasp the pidgin English. If only they would speak a bit slower, he could attempt to make sense of their conversation.

"Stefan, Ada means first daughter. My parents and close relatives call me Ada. Uzoma is my given name, my native name, and Augusta is my middle name."

"Now you know, sir; I'm referring to the girl beside you, Uzoma. Do you like her?" Ifeoma pushed. She'd always been an impulsive one and derives pleasure from such awkward scenarios. Uzoma knew she'd be hearty, unsettling Stefan in the manner she did, but she couldn't love her any less because she knew that beneath the facade, Ifeoma genuinely cared about her. Stefan turned to Uzoma, who was visibly blushing, obviously uncomfortable. It made his heart gloat.

"I do care about her a great deal," he answered more for Uzoma's benefit than his assailant.

"Please do not break her heart. Although she won't admit this, she hardly opens her heart to people. If you made it to this point, then, it means she likes you. She is more than delicate…"

"Babe abeg, go sleep, e don do…" Uzoma disconnected the call feeling ashamed.

"Ignore her please, she can be a pain sometimes."

"I meant what I said, Uzoma, or should I call you Ada, you mean a lot to me." Stefan lowered his lips and claimed hers. Uzoma tried resisting for some seconds, then gave in to the pleasure that surged through her entire being. She had been kissed before. She'd done most things with Ugochukwu except penetration, but now she found herself electrified by this kiss. It could be the long years of celibacy or it could be the result of her deepest yearning that made her body tremble. Whatever it was, she was lost in the universe momentarily, having no care at all. Unconsciously, she ran her fingers down his spine as she savored the moment in his arms.

"I've been longing to do that all day," Stefan muttered breathlessly, earning him a smile from his lassie. She was pleased their kiss had the same effect on him as it did on her.

"Uzoma, Ada, please date me, allow this white mule, this wandering urchin, to be your boyfriend."

Uzoma kissed him, devouring his mouth with her tongue until he gave in to another round of pleasure. "That's my response," she said and hugged him.

Chapter 9

Stefan was exceptionally gleeful, he felt like he'd won a lottery. That night, he couldn't sleep. He plotted places and things he would do with Uzoma, which restaurant he could take her to and what sort of foods she would like. He searched the internet for Nigerian restaurants in Gothenburg, the city they lived in and found none around them. He wasn't sure if she could eat traditional Swedish foods.

"Maybe she'll prefer Chinese, women tend to like Chinese food," he thought, then remembered that Uzoma was different from all the women he'd been with. He didn't know what to expect of her nor how she expected him to behave. He felt uneasy. He wasn't certain she'd appreciate constant calls or messages. The uncertainty unsettled him. While he brooded, his phone chimed: a text message from Uzoma. They had finally exchanged numbers with their relationship kicking off.

"Hej, thanks for today, boyfriend."

"Was thinking about you. We have a lot to talk about," Stefan replied.

"Things like?"

"About us, I don't want to get on your wrong side."

"Didn't know I was that scary. OK. We can talk tomorrow evening, I've assignments to do in the morning."

"Cool."

"My place or yours? Do you live alone?" Uzoma asked.

"No, I don't. I'll meet you at your place by four if you don't mind."

Stefan felt a little relieved. He would clear it all up with her the next day.

Uzoma had Egusi soup and Eba ready when Stefan got to her house. She wanted him to connect with her in deeper ways.

"This is Egusi soup. It is made of ground melon seeds, dried fish, meat, and palm oil; while this is Eba, it is processed cassava," Uzoma explained. She made the food a little spicy because she intended to induce him to eat spicy foods. She taught him to eat the meal with his hands.

"There's a saying: natural cutlery gives a better taste of the food," she coaxed.

Uzoma ate from the same plate as Stefan, which was new to him. This time, they ate on her little dining table. She encouraged him to eat more food, feeding him little pieces of meat. Stefan was amazed, he'd never experienced anything like he was experiencing at that moment, eating from the same plate with another person and with his bare hands.

"How was it?" Uzoma asked. "Be honest, how do you feel? I know this is all new to you and you're scared of offending me, but tell me exactly how you feel. It'll be better if we're open to each other."

"The food was a little spicy, thankfully I could manage, and eating with you felt lovely."

She kissed him.

"I understand that I'm not like every other girl you've dated before, I've also never dated a white guy. We'll have new experiences and navigate through this relationship together. We can also try the things you like and…"

Stefan shut her mouth with a kiss. How could she

understand his struggles so easily?

"What is your favorite color?" he queried.

"I'm not sure I have a favorite color. Sometimes I like red, yellow, or blue. I think it depends mostly on my mood."

He began to kiss her again, fondling with her buttons until she pulled away.

"Stefan, I promised to be open to you. Whatever we do, I do not want sex, at least not now. Maybe sometime in the future." She studied the expression on his face.

"It's not that I don't desire you, because I do, I just haven't crossed that phase in my life yet. I will with time. I hope this won't come between us."

"My fiery queen is a virgin," Stefan laughed, nibbling her fingers. "Sex won't separate us. I'll wait till you're ready." He knew it would be tormenting but he was willing to do anything to keep her. She provoked feelings in him deeper than he anticipated. He wouldn't trade that for anything, not even for his steaming desire to bed her.

She asked him about his parents and the lady he was with at the park. He also told her about his closest friends, Peder and Anders.

"Should I get my own apartment?" Stefan asked suddenly. "I want you to be able to visit me and feel comfortable." He knew he could receive visitors in his parents' home, but he was concerned about her. He wanted her to be happy. He'd never felt such a strong desire to please anyone before.

"No, Stefan. If you want to get an apartment because you want to move out of your parents' home, you can do that. Don't move out because of me. It is not necessary. If we want some privacy, we can use this apartment."

The following weekend, Stefan went for dinner with

Uzoma, Peder and Anders. Uzoma had taken time to apply her makeup and park her braids in a unique way, rolling them in three folds to achieve her African grandeur. Regardless of how people perceived her, she was proud of her color and her race. She wanted Stefan's friends to approve of her, to see the beauty in her.

Peder warmed up to her. They talked about Nigeria, about the weather and the peculiarities of her people. They talked about music, she recommended some popular hits and even played some on her phone for him. They bonded as friends. Anders kept quiet most of the evening. The few times he addressed Uzoma directly, his voice was raw with emotions of disdain and mostly to reprimand her. When they came to pick her up, Uzoma had kidded that she wanted to drive them. Stefan willingly handed the keys to her while Peder joked about their safety.

"Do you have a Swedish driving license? It's not enough to know how to drive," Anders cautioned, devoid of feelings. Uzoma handed the keys back to Stefan feeling downcast. Stefan appealed to Anders through a text message to act nicely and that made him become taciturn, completely withdrawn. Stefan was caught between the storm, his unfeeling childhood friend willing to ruin the evening, and his girlfriend who he knew could discern the scorn. He was thankful that Peder strived to make her happy. Stefan cared about Uzoma so much but was concerned about his decades of friendship with Anders. He understood his friend's uneasiness but still expected him to try for his sake.

As Uzoma played some Nigerian music with Peder on their way out of the restaurant, Anders tossed the last sword.

"Don't you think the music is quite loud? You shouldn't

disturb others," he chided.

Stefan had gone to pull the car from the parking lot. Peder hadn't defended her either, he simply kept mute. Uzoma excused herself, crossed over to the shopping complex across the road and disappeared.

Uzoma had been scorned severally in the past. She'd learnt that people reacted in different ways to strangers. She was even taught the concept of strangeness as a topic in intercultural communication course in class, yet she hoped that Stefan's friends would be different, dreamed of amazing moments with them and craved to cook her local dishes for them. She had asked her mom to send her some dried snails and had imagined making a bowl of snails in a sauce for all of them to eat together on a cool evening while watching a Swedish comedy.

It was in moments like this that she wished Ifeoma had come with her to Sweden. Ifeoma would have taught Anders a lesson he'd never forget. She always knew the right things to say in such situations. She smiled as she remembered the tart Ifeoma fed the bus preacher that harassed her over her dressing on their way back from school one day. The preacher had used Uzoma as an example of wayward girls, indicating that her gown was short and she would go to hell for it. Ifeoma had shouted "preach it pastor" from the back seat and the man had thanked her, thinking he was making an impact.

"Sir, does your daughter, sister, or anyone in your family dress like this?" Ifeoma inquired and the preacher negated then boasted about the perfect behavior of his children. Ifeoma praised his virtuousness and his kindness for trying to correct the children of others.

"But sir, your girls must be in heaven now," she added,

baffling the preacher

"Yes, now," she continued, "if they were so perfect, they must be in heaven already. If they are still on earth, then it means that their perfect dressing hasn't gotten them to heaven either. You were even boasting about it, Pastor. Did you never read in your bible? 'It is by grace that we are saved through faith, not of works lest any man should boast.' It didn't say by dressing shall ye make heaven. My condolences to your children for having such a demeaning father." There was an uproar as everyone on the bus applauded Ifeoma while the preacher sat silently for the rest of the journey.

"If only Ifeoma were here," Uzoma muttered to herself.

Uzoma pulled out her phone and dialed her sister. Ifeoma did not pick up. She felt lonely, very lonely. She saw Stefan's calls and muted them. She wasn't in the mood to speak with him, not at the moment. Her relationship was only one week old, officially, and the storms were here already. She wondered if the relationship would survive. Friends influence each other and the trio has been together most of their lives. She wouldn't want to come between them.

Neither Uzoma nor Stefan had professed love yet. She knew she had strong feelings for Stefan, felt different each time he kissed her, but could it be love? Could such love surmount racial bias? Where was their relationship headed anyway? Would her parents allow their only child to get married to a foreigner and live in a foreign land for most of her life? She couldn't imagine such an outcome, so she decided to live for the moment. She wouldn't allow Anders to influence her choices. If she would break up with Stefan, it would be on her terms and not because of another. Consoled, she went home.

Chapter 10

Stefan waited patiently for Uzoma by her doorstep. He tried all he could to remain calm. He was ignorant of what transpired between his friends and Uzoma that made her bolt away and, worse still, ignore his calls. He knew Anders had maligned Uzoma all evening, but he couldn't fathom the exact matter that led to her disappearance. Peder had only offered his apologies when he returned to pick them up, while Anders kept mute. If he knew the evening would go awry, he'd have spent it with Uzoma alone. Peder had insisted on meeting with her and Stefan was confident his friends would marvel at her astounding personality. Now he could only hope that whatever had transpired would not be the death of his relationship that was only just kicking off. He paced a little and returned to his initial position at her doorpost. Thanks to the long hours of work at the factory that required him to stand most of the time, his wait was not enervating. Glancing at his wristwatch over and over, he rehearsed an apology speech. He would try his best to ensure that his relationship survived the hiccup.

"Hi, querida," Uzoma said casually when she got home and hugged him.

"I'm so sorry, I didn't know you were waiting for me. I should give you a key to avoid this next time." She opened the door and walked in, leaving the perplexed Stefan watching, wondering what she was up to.

"Are you hungry? Because I'm famished. We could eat together," she uttered and disappeared into her sleeping area to undress. They had dinner at the restaurant with Peder and Anders but the long walk sapped her strength, leaving her bowel empty. She was trying to act all right, yet Stefan knew she wasn't. He could feel the strain in her voice. He knew something was eating her deep inside. Her hug lacked its usual warmth. Something was wrong and whatever it was, she wasn't ready to fight it, or she would have been spitting fire. She wasn't his fiery queen for nothing. He walked into her sleeping area and hugged her from behind.

"You know you can talk to me. Please let it out." He wanted to know all that transpired in his absence, he wanted her to react. He was ready to accept the blame and apologize. He didn't want her bottling things up, it could affect her feelings for him. Although they had never professed their love, he could tell she felt something for him. He wouldn't want anything to jeopardize that. He turned her to face him.

"What happened?"

"Nothing that hasn't happened before," she replied and broke out of his embrace to get them food. They ate silently while he observed her. She was shutting him out of her pains. Whatever Anders had said to her had done some damage.

"Please talk to me, Ada," he pleaded, taking her hand in his to coax her.

"Nothing serious. At least his opinion of me was correct. I am loud, very loud, and I do not pretend to be otherwise. At least he saw something that was factual." She smiled dolefully, a tear escaping her eyes.

"When I got admission to school here," she continued, "in dire need of accommodation, I rented a bigger apartment, two rooms through the online site, Blocket. After I got here, I decided to exchange the apartment, *bostad byte*, for a smaller one. Luckily, I got this place. A woman from Kosovo lived here. After we agreed on the terms, she repeatedly drummed it into my ears to keep my former apartment clean, especially the toilet. She said she was a very neat person and would not tolerate dirty toilets. She even called me on the phone a day before we moved to wash the toilet. When I moved in here, I realized that her 'super clean toilet' had stains at the bottom. I had to pour chlorine into the toilet to get out the stains because they were very irritating to me. My former apartment was a new one, the toilet and bath very new as well and had no stain whatsoever. I was the first tenant, while this one was built in the '70s. I wondered why she said that to me when she couldn't keep her toilet clean. She left her waste bin and a rag behind as a gift to me," Uzoma paused, inhaling deeply. "That woman judged me without knowing me. The color of my skin told her I was a dirty pig, so she felt the need to warn me to be clean. So you see, Anders judged me on something that was true, how can I fault him?"

Stefan felt his heart torn apart for her sake. He couldn't imagine the pains she was going through. He drew her closer to himself and hugged her, caressing her. He lacked words to assuage her feelings. He felt so sad. He'd always met her apartment neat and tidied. She was a perfectionist, so much so that objects were aligned properly all the time. How could anyone associate the word dirt with her? Suddenly the things she said to him the first day they met felt light. He couldn't even imagine why she decided to date him despite all she had been through and he imagined there were many more he didn't know. If verbal expressions of feelings were therapeutic, he would absorb her pains and bring her healing. He would be a shoulder for her to lean on and offer his ears to her to relieve those moments. He would mend her heart and feelings.

"It's late," Uzoma declared. "Do you want to go home or stay here?"

"I'll stay if you'll have me."

"Sure!"

Uzoma gave him a spare toothbrush to use and a new towel. She ransacked her box, searching earnestly. Stefan was glad to see her become lively again. She seemed keen to have him. He went to his car to pick up the overnight bag he usually kept there, which he used mostly when he crashed at his friends'. Uzoma was pacing around when he returned.

"You disappeared. I was wondering where you went to." He could see the worry in her eyes dissipate. She truly cared about him. His decision to spend the night had cheered her. He knew it would be a long night, especially with her no-sex condition. He heaved a sigh of relief, at least she had become her usual self again.

"Just had to pick up my overnight bag from the car. I keep it for moments like this."

He watched her shoulders drop.

"I got this out for you." She pointed to a brown silky drape. "It is called a Jelabia. It's a common dressing among the Hausas in Nigeria. It's unisex. I have two of them and this is new, so it's OK."

"Hey, relax, fiery queen. I don't mind wearing the one you've worn before as long as it is yours. I am not touchy. It looks like you're judging me for being white," he smiled at her.

"Guilty as charged," she responded, covering her face

with her hands. She had imagined whites as perfect people and the western world, a perfect place. She'd heard her granny and many others say "bekee bu agbara", which meant 'whites are gods.' A fallacious concept embedded in her people from a tender age that made them only yearn to be like the whites. She'd seen people give up lucrative jobs just to travel to the white man's land and regardless of what life meted out to them in the foreign land, they remained for the prestige and the adoration gotten from people at home. The opinion of family members living in white man's land was superior to that of those at home simply because they had mingled with the whites and so were deemed wiser. White people in her country were treated like kings, employed as expatriates, and were paid higher than the citizens. Those with certificates from the white man's land were considered for jobs before those with local certificates irrespective of their abilities, the reason many families send their children abroad for studies and her family was guilty as well. Those who had been abroad were treated as ajebutter, despite the fact that the person could have been living in the ghetto area of the white man's land. [4] Only that people at home were ignorant of the fact that white man's land also had ghettos and villages. Uzoma was shocked to discover the living conditions of many of her people when she first arrived, yet sadly, many of them would visit home acting as kings to the envy of the locals. She wished people at home would know the truth. Regardless, she found herself treating Stefan as a king, as an ajebutter. Schemas were difficult to override.

Uzoma beckoned to Stefan to use the bathroom first just

---

[4] rich and spoilt and cannot withstand any form of suffering

so she could tidy up after herself. Both of them felt awkward, Stefan in the drape a few inches above his ankle, but he liked it, the material, the design on the neck region, and the free fall. Uzoma admired him also, the jelabia looked good on him.

"I'll ask my mother to send a longer one. You'll look better in a longer one that gets to your ankle," she panted nervously. Standing close to him made her breathless.

Stefan pulled her into an embrace. He knew what she dreaded, the sleeping arrangements.

"Fiery queen, I want you to relax. You can go to bed and sleep. I'll sleep on the sofa. I promised I won't do anything you don't approve of. I won't touch you. I respect your wishes."

"If you're certain, then let's sleep on the same bed," she offered.

Who were they kidding? They knew they wouldn't get any sleep if they went to bed together out of self-consciousness.

"Let's watch a movie," Uzoma suggested instead and occupied her favorite position on the floor with her blanket. Stefan sat behind her cuddling her as they watched Solsidan. Uzoma felt she could connect with the character of Anna in the comedy as Anna tried to fit in among her spouse's family and friends in a new environment.

Chapter 11

Uzoma invited Stefan to Crystabel's second birthday party. The party would be an African affair and attended mostly by Africans. Everything about the party including the music and food would be African — Nigerian. Uzoma and Stefan had bonded in the last few weeks. They forged a pattern in their relationship. They spent their weekends together. While Stefan created masterly designs for his work, he was swift with his pencil and loved to draw, Uzoma read her books in the companionable silence of her man. In the evenings, they watched movies or visited the malls. The weather had gotten chilly, so Uzoma preferred the comfort and warmth of her home.

It was only fair she invited him to the party so that they could still spend the day together, though in the company of others. She couldn't decline her invitation because Crystabel's mother, Aisha, was her friend and had been good to her. Besides, she loved Crystabel very much, too. Uzoma intimated Stefan on possible expectations at the party, loud music, drinks, food, and dance. She knew Stefan might be uncomfortable at the party, but a secret affair wasn't her idea of a relationship. She wanted the Nigerian community to know her man. She had initially turned down a few relationship requests from some of the men of her race, because she dreaded dating another proud or egocentric man like

Ugochukwu. She'd love to read their expressions over her choice of a partner. She knew tongues would wag and looked forward to it.

The idea of attending the party was somewhat unsettling for Stefan. It could be the concept of strangeness or from his inexperience of such parties. From Uzoma's description, he could tell of impending differentiations from the parties he had attended in the past. He had never been to any African party and from Uzoma's supposition, he might be the only white person in their midst. He knew his demeanor would be observed and judged and he wasn't sure what an appropriate behavior would be in this instance.

"Just be yourself querida," Uzoma encouraged.

Stefan only agreed to the party to please Uzoma. Moreover, he reckoned that his relationship would be solidified if he learned more about the peculiarities of his inamorata. He was glad she extended her invitation to him but dreaded the occasion. He loved Uzoma more than he ever loved any other. Although he was yet to voice his feelings, he had shown her in every way he could how much she meant to him. Stefan spent time with his friends, during weekdays, at work, and during breaks, but rarely visited or crashed in their apartment any more. He slept at home on weekdays to compensate his parents for his absence on weekends. His parents understood his feelings, he was their child and they knew the gliding effects of love. He decorated his room with Uzoma's pictures and spoke to her every evening to enable him to manage his feelings when he wasn't with her. They were still not sexually involved, but they'd learned to appreciate each other's company regardless.

Stefan was distraught over Uzoma's unwillingness to

inform her parents of their relationship. She stilled him whenever she responded to their calls and denied being in any relationship when her aunt in the UK asked her. Stefan thought she was ashamed of him or worse still of his race.

"Bae, I'm simply waiting for the right time to inform them. If I told my mom or aunt, they wouldn't sit still, they would want to see you," she explained. "It's not that I do not want them to meet you, but in all honesty, they would worry if they knew I was dating a white guy," Stefan had felt even more frustrated. He'd never imagined his skin color could be an impediment in any of his relationships. He loved her too much to quit.

"My parents would fret that I would fall in love and marry you and…"

"What's wrong with that?" Stefan asked angrily.

"There is nothing wrong with that. They would worry because I'm their only child, marrying a white man would mean living far away from home. It'll break them."

Stefan didn't understand the difference. She was in his country, already far away from home, so what could be different and what does it matter anyway? He'd picked up his car keys to leave her apartment, but she stopped him.

"Stefan, please understand," she pleaded, her fear evident in her eyes. She was scared of losing him. She was almost tearing up.

"I'm sorry I lied to my aunt. I did it because I didn't want her to come to Sweden to 'straighten' me up." She narrated her mother's traditional stance about a single lady living alone and her choice of UK schools for her so she could live under her aunt's watchful eyes.

"Stefan, I promise, if it was that easy, I'd have told them.

They might even ask me to return home if I tell them. Besides, Stefan, our relationship is still young. If and when the time comes and we choose to spend the rest of our lives together, we'll visit Nigeria together and inform them properly. It'll be easier to explain to them and make them understand in person." She had hugged him tightly, pleading until his anger softened. He had a weakness for her agony, the sorrowful reflection on her face had immobilized him. Uzoma ensured that Stefan spoke with Ifeoma every weekend instead so he could connect with someone close to her. Her decision to attend the birthday party with Stefan was to popularize their relationship and confer on him a sense of security. Stefan felt Uzoma's invitation was her way of creating more room for him and acknowledging their relationship.

At the party, Uzoma was busy assisting Aisha in the kitchen and attending to the other party guests. Stefan ensconced himself between a brawny looking man dressed in blue jeans, white jumper, and adorned with gold necklace, bangle, and wristwatch; and a slender, petite, and vivacious lady, both Nigerians. Stefan was happy he wasn't the only white person at the party. A Polish lady married to a Nigerian was there with her three children. Stefan made an acquaintance with her. She seemed well suited amidst black folks and mingled easily, hugging and greeting most of the guests. Observing her, Stefan hoped for a time he'd feel so free in the midst of such company. He wanted deeply to believe his relationship with Uzoma would lead to something more lasting, but Uzoma had been on the fence, insisting on the moment. He craved for her love, that she would love him as much as he loved her.

"I am Idara," the girl sitting beside Stefan declared,

extending her hand and interrupting Stefan's thoughts.

"Stefan." He granted her a handshake.

Uzoma appeared several times to gratify Stefan's wants, offering him her choice of food and drink while Idara kept him occupied with tales and questions.

"Let's dance, I'm certain your girlfriend won't mind," Idara proposed. She was so insistent that Stefan gave in. He knew he couldn't dance to the beats in the same way the other men at the party did, but he didn't want to lose Idara's company. She was so flexible and a great dancer, moving her arsenal in a seductive manner. Stefan grew weary of the situation. He observed that they were generating interest. Uzoma appeared, smiled at him, and disappeared into the kitchen. He felt uneasy. He was almost certain someone had called Uzoma's attention to his undertaking with Idara. He apologized to Idara and sat down feeling more awkward.

"So, you and Uzoma are an item," the man on Stefan's right inquired.

"She's my girlfriend."

"Be careful, man, don't allow her to use you and dump you. Very soon she'll be through with her studies and would need someone to assist her with the extension of her permit. Be careful. This is from one man to another, and I know our people," the man advised.

Stefan became gloomy for the rest of the evening, wondering why the man deemed it fit to warn him. His father's words echoed in his head. He had said the same thing. What was he missing? What could they see that he couldn't see? Was he blinded by his feelings for her and he couldn't see through her act?

"Can I have your number?" Idara asked. "I just want to be

your friend. Who knows, I might need your assistance tomorrow, or you mine. It's a small world, you'll never know what tomorrow will be." Stefan declined out of loyalty to Uzoma. Besides, his feelings at that moment were conflicted. He was upset. Was Uzoma really using him?

The man who had spoken to Stefan approached Uzoma in the hallway.

"I can see who you chose over me. Do you think he can grind you like us? These people eat vegetables, we eat correct poundo, their stamina cannot match ours," the man boasted and Uzoma laughed.

"You're right," Uzoma whispered. "But he is ten times the man you'll ever be and I'll choose him a thousand times over you." She gave him a pat and walked to Stefan. She bent down and kissed him to the glaring eyes of many keen on observing them.

"Let's go," she said and matched out with him.

Uzoma noticed Stefan's cold and reclusive mood. She didn't know what was eating him up. She had seen Idara flirting with him, he even danced with her. She should be the one upset and not Stefan.

"I'm going home tonight, I'll see you," Stefan said as he dropped her off. It was a Saturday, Stefan always stayed with her all through the weekend. She was certain something was wrong and he didn't seem inclined to speak with her about it. Uzoma tried to protest but he insisted.

"Please respect my decision," he said coldly. She got out of his car and he left.

Chapter 12

For five days, Uzoma neither heard from nor spoke with Stefan. He wouldn't pick up her calls nor respond to her messages. She realized how shallow their relationship had been. She neither knew his place nor any of his friend's places. She had never asked. She didn't even have Peder's number. She had seen neither Peder nor Anders after the ordeal that led to her walking out on them. She had never bothered, Stefan had been there every other weekend. She enjoyed their solitude. She felt so frustrated having no one to turn to at this time.

"Whatever it is, we can talk about it." She had sent this message several times to Stefan, tweaking it in different ways. She felt so lonely. She confided in Ifeoma. She thought Idara had gotten to Stefan. She wanted to fight her for him. Uzoma had seen the way Idara regarded her man on the day of the party. She had been happy rather than jealous because she was delighted that her man was cute enough to be admired by others. She was proud of him. Uzoma restrained herself from being impolite in her messages to Stefan as much as she wanted to taunt him for flirting with Idara and giving her an attitude afterwards. She even pleaded with him to visit her, to answer her calls, or even to respond to her messages.

Stefan felt heartbroken. He needed time to sort his feelings for Uzoma. Encouraging any form of intimacy or a close affinity with her would jeopardize his evaluation and entangle him with his emotions. His father had warned him about her, Anders also, then an unknown man of her race, from her country. Even a dimwit could see the imprints of wisdom in their admonition. If his father and Anders were blinded by their racial prejudice, what of the man at the party? She had never confessed love for him, rather she had insisted on no sexual relationship and acted like a prude. She could have been pretending. Maybe she didn't perceive him as worthy enough for such intimacy. She wouldn't discuss the future, as though she knew their relationship would end. That could explain her inability to disclose their relationship to her parents or her aunt. All that excuse about colors and him being white could have been a diversion to foster her ploy. She had never been inquisitive about him, had never asked to visit him or asked anything about his family. Suddenly, everything began to fall into place. She must have planned it and he had fallen into her trap. Stefan felt excruciating pain. He had never perceived himself as a half-witted person. He couldn't confide in anyone because he felt silly for not seeing what was glaring to everyone. He picked up the jelabia Uzoma had given him, he couldn't bring himself to discard it. She probably gave him gifts to entice him.

"Something that will steal your heart," she had said to him the first day they cooked together, and she was right, she did steal his heart. What a fool he had been. The signs were there, he should have known better. He was blinded by his quest for love and had ignored all the alarms. He resolved to end things with her.

On Thursday evening, Stefan heard the doorbell ring. He was in the kitchen. His parents were home. They weren't expecting any visitors. His grandparents wouldn't call at their house by eight p.m., nor would any of his friends visit without prior notice or a call. The doorbell rang twice again and his parents came downstairs curious. His mother opened the door and recognized Uzoma instantly. She had seen her picture in Stefan's room. She also knew her son had been suffering from heartache in the past few days.

"Good evening, ma'am, I'm sorry to barge in on you like this and at this hour but I really need to see Stefan," Uzoma expressed. She had gotten Stefan's address online. She was tired of crying and decided to confront him. If he wasn't keen on continuing with the relationship, she'd return the belongings he left in her house and nurse her broken heart. Stefan heard her voice at the door and began to pace around. His father encouraged him to listen to Uzoma since she took the pains to seek him out. He signaled to his mother to let her in.

"If you wanted to end things with me, you should be brave enough to tell me so," Uzoma started as soon as she saw Stefan.

"Good evening, sir," she greeted Stefan's father before turning back to Stefan. She was so hurt and in no mood for decorum.

"I saw you flirting with Idara at the party. I should be the one upset here, not you. Or have you decided to date Idara instead? If that were the case, you should have told me."

"Idara has nothing to do with this," Stefan defended. "I discovered your plans."

"What plans? What are you talking about?"

"People close to me tried to warn me but I didn't listen. I thought they were judging you because of your color, I thought they were being racially biased towards you," he paused taking a deep breath. "I found out they were not. I should have listened to them."

"Stefan, what the heck are you talking about?"

"The guy that sat beside me at the party, the one you were chatting with just before we left, told me the same thing."

"That?" Uzoma asked, impatiently.

"That you were using me for papers. That all you wanted from me was a resident permit after which you would dump me." Uzoma was speechless for a couple of seconds then she burst into laughter. She dialed a number on her phone and put the phone on speaker.

"Hello, Micheal. How are you?" she said as calmly as she could.

"This one you're calling me today, have you realized your mistake? Or has your oyibo boyfriend dumped you?" Micheal answered sarcastically.

"Micheal, do you still want to date me?" Uzoma asked in a low seductive tone.

"Have you finally come to your senses? I don't know what you saw in that white guy. What does he have that we don't have? I heard you turned down Izuchukwu too. If you don't want to date me because I'm from Edo state, what of Izuchukwu? He is your Igbo brother. Girl, we've been in this country long before you. We know these people better. That guy go use and dump you. Receive sense, Sister."

"Is that why you told him I was using him for papers?"

"Abi, I lie, you're using him for papers now."

"Micheal, do you know the main reason I didn't date you? Because you were flaunting your citizenship before me and I detest proud men. And regardless of what you do to separate

Stefan and me, I'll never date you. I called to say thank you, I can see your handiwork, you've done well. Like I told you at the party, he's a thousand times the man you'll ever be."

Uzoma disconnected the call and sighed.

"So, this is the reason you've been acting this way. Wow, it means you believe it. Oh, I forgot, you said people close to you warned you as well, maybe it's time you listened to them."

"Ada, do you really care about me? You won't discuss anything about the future with me. You won't tell your family about me. You act like our relationship will end soon."

"You're right, Stefan. I do not see a future with you yet. What will this future be? Marriage? Will my mother survive it? I am here in this country at this time because she believes it's only for studies, that I'll soon be home. And do you know how many months it took me to prevail on her to allow me to study here? You're right Stefan. I gave us a chance because I believed in love, I believed that if our love could be strong enough, it might surmount every barrier, but I guess I was mistaken. You asked if I cared about you, if everything I've done since we started dating cannot answer that, then nothing will." She wiped the tears that escaped from her eye. Stefan was dumbfounded. He wanted to go to her, to hold her, to apologize, but his feet stalled.

"Here, Stefan. Your things are in the bag. It's OK if you don't want to see me again. I'll survive. I wish you well." She dropped the bag on the table, wore her shoes, and left the house. Stefan was transfixed. Suddenly he burst into tears, allowing the anguish of the past days to cascade. He had allowed his imagination to cost him his relationship. He should have followed his heart, should have trusted her, should have believed in what they shared. He should have stopped her from leaving, he should have apologized to her, he should have told her how much he loved her, but he didn't, he simply watched. Now it was too late, he had lost her. He wept uncontrollably. His mother patted him on his back, mollifying him.

"Go to her Stefan," she cooed.

Chapter 13

Uzoma's heart was throbbing as she sat down at the bus stop in the chilly grasp of winter. It was past ten p.m. and the public transportation intervals were stretched. According to the information box, she would need to wait another forty minutes for the next bus. She sat on the public bench as her heart wrenched over her broken relationship. She blamed herself for attending the party with Stefan. She blamed the unknown people in Stefan's life for sowing loathsome seeds in him. She believed Anders must be one of the culprits. She blamed Micheal for his retribution, such a loser. He'd never have her, even if he were the last man on earth. Uzoma blamed Stefan for his lack of trust in her. How could he be so easily swayed? A Swedish permanent resident permit had never been on her agenda because she knew that harboring such thoughts was like building castles in the air. It would be difficult to convince her parents to allow her to settle in a foreign land far away from home. Would she survive it herself? She had only been away from home for sixteen months and it seemed like ages to her. She missed home, mostly now since she had severed her relationship. She broke down in tears, her body freezing as much as her heart, feeling so lonely. If only Ifeoma had come with her to Sweden. She should have convinced her parents to sponsor Ifeoma. She looked up and saw no stars. Were they mocking her as well? Have they abandoned her too? In

Nigeria, she had always spoken to the stars whenever she was alone, but she had never been outside and alone at night in Sweden, at least not long enough to check on her night sky pals. Maybe she abandoned them first. She needed to get home, to wake up from this slumber. Who would have thought that Stefan, her Stefan, a white guy, the same man who chose to spend his weekends with her rather than his family or his bosom friends, could be so easily swayed? And even if she truly wanted to get a permanent resident permit through him, was that a lot to ask of one's boyfriend? She trusted him, a little too much maybe, or she wouldn't have been so disappointed.

Stefan got to Uzoma's house and let himself in with the spare key she had given him. She didn't collect the key when she came to their house. It provided a perfect excuse for his visit, as he wondered what to say to her when she returned. He sat on the settee feeling like an intruder. Where was she? He glanced at the wall clock and began to pace around impatiently. What had he done? How did he allow a stranger to come between them? How did he allow his sentiments to cloud his judgment? He felt senile. He'd always taken his decisions himself and made independent judgments, now he allowed others to influence his actions. What would Uzoma think of him? God, he mustn't lose her. He had allowed a stranger, a rival, to come between them. She had favored him, chosen him, and he had let her down sadly.

Uzoma walked in almost an hour later looking sick, shivering from the cold. She had not expected to see Stefan at home, it was home for both of them, for her house was their love nest, and it gladdened her heart.

"Good evening," she offered to Stefan, dashing away into

the bathroom as though she had only chanced upon an unpleasant housemate she must tolerate. She needed a hot bath; her hands and feet were becoming numb. Would she ever get used to Swedish cold weather? Besides, skimming off into the bathroom would buy her some much needed time to coordinate her thoughts. She was not ready to face Stefan, not yet, not at the moment. She had wished he'd be there when she got home, even hoped, yet she was unprepared. She knew his presence at this time would only mean he wanted to apologize for his folly, but she had no intentions of making it easy for him. She was after all a woman and would derive joy from watching him attempt to amend things. What if he had come just to return her key? The thought horrified her. If that was his intent, she should at least give them a chance at conversation to see if she could salvage their relationship. Thoughts of losing him dreaded her. What if she tarried in the bathroom only to meet his absence later? She got out of the shower, dried her body, and strutted out with the towel around her, covering her naked body. It was her house after all and she could do as she pleased. Stefan was still there, sitting on the settee, she noted, stifling a smile. But for the cold weather, she would have worn seductive nightwear. She could leverage her femininity to get her much deserved apology. There must be something she could wear to feel sassy. She rummaged through her things and decided on a teal green jumper and black leggings that clung to her body, revealing her curves. She walked out and dished food for herself, not bothering with him. He wasn't a stranger, she thought, he is physically fit to help himself if he was hungry.

"Ada, please can we talk?" Stefan pleaded. His patience was weaning. He knew she was deliberately ignoring him and he deserved it. He joined Uzoma on the table and held her left hand while she ate with the right. He thought she would object or react, but like a meek lamb, she let him have his way while she concentrated on her food, ignoring him.

"I'm sorry," he apologized, and Uzoma ignored him. She finished her meal and set out to do the dishes.

"Please talk to me, Ada. I'm so sorry that I hurt you," Stefan begged, hugging her from behind. She flinched at his touch, a wave of sensation warming up her body. How could she stay angry with him when her body and heart betrayed her so?

"What exactly are you sorry about?" Uzoma asked, barely audible, not for lack of strength but the sensation caused by his body positioned behind her and his hands caressing her biceps made her dreamy. He was careful not to allow his hands to stray as much as he wanted to. He wasn't sure about the state of their relationship yet. At least she hadn't turned him away yet.

"I'm sorry for everything. I should have trusted you. I shouldn't have listened to that man nor anyone else. I should have trusted what we have."

"Stefan, so if I wanted a Swedish resident permit as your girlfriend, you'd have dumped me rather than help me? Why would I date a white guy for it when I could have dated any of the black Swedes and still achieve the same result? I'm not even certain I want to stay back in this country yet and you guys seem to have decided for me."

"I'm sorry, Ada, please. And even if you decide to stay back in the country after your studies, I can help with the permit, just don't throw me into the woods." Now, the idea of helping with the permit by simply acknowledging their relationship seemed trivial to him. How did the same issue affect him all the much more than it did earlier? Then it dawned on him: it wasn't the resident permit that rallied him, it was his solemn desire to win her love and the fear she could end things with him if she had any ulterior motives that got fulfilled. Oh, he would give much more than a resident permit if she would love him. How he longed to hear her say those three words, to profess love for him because then, he would freely express his feelings to her and love her without reservation.

"Stefan," she turned to face him, "you mean the world to me. I know you gave in to pressures from your loved ones because I refused to discuss what tomorrow could be with you. The reason I do not speak about the future is because I know not what it holds. My culture is a little more complicated than yours, I cannot just take decisions without the consent of my parents, it will break their hearts. Maybe I could do that if I had other siblings and damn their feelings, but I can't, it will kill them. I just want us to thread carefully, live one day at a time, that way we can surmount every challenge, together." Even at this moment, Uzoma hadn't promised anything but Stefan felt reassured. She was willing to fight for them, that they may overcome challenges together. He bent down and claimed her lips with his, blanking out the world.

Chapter 14

Does the river always flow in seamless waves?

Do tides forever remain?

Can smiles and laughter in a soul nest?

And can pearls upon a feet glamour?

Uzoma was familiar with the saying, "life is not a bed of roses," and like many, she wanted to write her own script, to create her own path, a beautiful path like her name signified. She wanted love, true love, limitless love, and fate seemed to have furnished her desire. She never wanted to be the Shakespearean Juliet because of the tragic death. She wanted a happy ending, happily ever after, yet she found herself caged, unable to think of the future. Not only for the dread of residing in a foreign land, for Sweden was indeed a beautiful country, nor for the dread of broaching the issue with her parents, for she was confident that although they might be tempestuous, her parents would eventually give in to her desire if it made her happy. She was their only child after all. Her dissension was fueled by the differences in their dispositions to life. Stefan was more individualistic in his approach to life. Not exactly selfish, independent rather, personalized. He wouldn't strain much over others, he walked with his decisions and expected everyone to respect them. After all, his life was his to live. Uzoma was grateful he cared enough for her to include her in his plans. Only he didn't want children. He wanted a life with his partner, his lover, void of any intrusions from the world. He believed being plagued with raising a child will drill his time and make him share his love, which he wasn't sure he was capable of, or he could end up worse than his parents, neglecting the child. He would rather not traumatize any child. He wanted to live his life free of such responsibilities. At the moment, Uzoma was central to him. And she was happy, very happy. Stefan filled her day and dreams and her joy flowed like the rivers.

Christmas brought along merry tidings of peace and love and she shared it with Stefan and his family in their home. Uzoma returned to her house on the twenty-eighth of December after her time with Stefan and his family. She was hearty, very hearty, looking forward to the new year and its glamour. Sometimes, thoughts of ever after with Stefan perched on her mind, but she wouldn't allow it to bloom. She was afraid of tomorrow, afraid her parents might give their blessings begrudgingly if she prevailed on them. And what would the future be for a man that wanted no child? He had told her of his intentions never to father a child as they watched one of their evening movies. She had asked if he meant his words and he had affirmed, looking grave enough to send a note of finality to her. A contrast to what she wanted. She wanted children, four or six, a large family. Uzoma had decidedly forbidden herself from brooding on this mark, believing that the bridge would be crossed at the right time.

Now at home alone, yet not lonely for she knew Stefan would soon call, she decided to call her parents and relations. Now, she had time to listen to gossip, the details of all happening in her hometown. The majority of her tribal men and women traveled home to their villages for Christmas. Her parents traveled to their village the previous day, two days after Christmas. They wanted to celebrate the new year at home with their extended family. Uzoma wished she was home. She missed the outings, visiting relatives, watching masquerades, visiting the streams, and other festivities usually organized by the youths in her hometown. Unlike Sweden, the streets would be buzzing and people would be out rather than indoors. Bush bars where animals like grasscutter were piquantly roasted and served with palm wine freshly tapped in the mornings and evenings were patronized. Her people really did have numerous meat delicacies. Her favorites were isi ewu made of goat head and nkwobi made of cow leg. Their tastes were heavenly and they were served in local calabash-like plates. She also enjoyed snails prepared in the sauce used for African salad. A local restaurant in her village that served it was usually filled to the brim with customers this season.

While bars would be filled with people, major junctions and village fields would be trafficked by pedestrians and vehicles. Some things were best experienced on foot, people would pack their vehicles even by the roadsides for the thrill of the masquerades, the fear, the race, and the joy that comes with the victory. Tradition forbade women from looking directly at the masquerade, but they looked anyway, though not when any was within reach for the fear of the long canes carried by the masquerades. Yet women and girls gloried in watching masquerades, especially in their competitive dance at the village square. Oh, how she missed home. She thought about the youth festivities, artist's performances, age-grade dances, the streams where she'd go with her cousins just to sit under the waterfall. Home was noisy, dusty from Harmattan during Christmas, and filled with delightful thrills.

Excited and desperately in need to connect to the activities at home, Uzoma called her mother. After several unpicked calls to her mother, Uzoma called her grandmother, her maternal grandmother. Her paternal grandmother had died four years earlier.

"Hello, Nne," Uzoma called her granny, excited.[5]

"Ugo m," her grandmother replied, groaning. Normally, her grandmother would shower her with praises. Ugo m, which meant 'my glory,' was just one out of many sweet names her grandmother would call her. Something was wrong. Her grandmother hadn't continued with her usual chatter. She even groaned! Something was certainly wrong. Uzoma's spirits dropped.

"What's wrong, Grandma?" she inquired in Igbo.

"Nothing." Her granny groaned again.

"Nne, I'm not a child any more. I can tell that something is wrong besides your groaning. Would you tell me or would you rather I hopped on the next flight home?" Uzoma threatened in English just so her granny would feel the depth of her sobriety.

"Your mother will tell you."

Uzoma bade her good health and disconnected the call. What could have happened? Did someone die? Her granny said her mother would tell her, which meant her mom was alive. "What of my dad?" she thought and began to panic.

She called her father and got no response. She called Ifeoma, again there was no response.

Uzoma decided to call her uncle, her father's only brother, his stepbrother, Ndukaku.

---

[5] Igbo name for mother

"Hello, Uncle. Merry Christmas."

"How are you?" Ndukaku replied.

"I'm awesome, uncle. I can't reach my parents, have you seen them?"

"Am I your parents' keeper? If you can't reach them, try again or go look for them," her uncle replied coldly and disconnected the call. Uzoma should have known better than to call her uncle. They had never been close. The uncle's wife, Ekemma, had been a louse on her mom's skin, tormenting Uzoma's mother for her failure to produce a male child. She seized every opportunity to rub it in and gloat about her three sons. Uzoma recalled the day her mom came home from the women's meeting exasperated. Ekemma had challenged her mother in front of everyone, opposing all her suggestions. And when Mmachi made a donation to the group, Ekemma had made a callous statement. She accused Mmachi of being a 'show off', declaring that Mmachi wasted money because she had no son to inherit it. A battle of words between Ekemma's supporters and Mmachi's loyalists followed. Mmachi had left the meeting sad and depressed over her plight. She was not a barren woman nor an unfaithful wife, her only crime was her inability to produce a male child. Now her sister-in-law assail her and even covet her husband's rightful inheritance because she had no son for him.

Mmachi had long since given up on the family's plantain plantation that was rightfully her husband's. Ekemma had coveted it on the claims that her children were to inherit the land. Mmachi knew she was right according to tradition, only that she could have waited for such a time when her children inherit the land before harvesting the proceeds. Mmachi tolerated Ekemma's excesses for peace to reign, she didn't fight over the plantation and had even dissuaded her husband from fighting over it because she was charitable. In reality, Uzoma's parents have no need for the plantation, they had more than enough to take care of their needs, unlike Ekemma's family who was barely making ends meet. Yet that hadn't satisfied her assailant. Uzoma knew all this. She knew how much ridicule her mother suffered from her uncle and his wife. How could she expect any good response from her uncle? At least, he hadn't declared any of her parents dead. He would have told her if any of them had died, or wouldn't he? She could only hope.

Chapter 15

"Your father…"

"What happened to my father? Is he dead?" Uzoma inquired, interrupting Ifeoma. She had got through to her that evening. Ifeoma had traveled to the village with Uzoma's parents and planned to leave for her own village from Uzoma's hometown just before the New year to see her people.

"No, of course not. But he is in the hospital. He had a minor heart attack."

Uzoma collapsed on the floor. Her father was healthy when she spoke to him the previous day. He even traveled to the village with her mom and Ifeoma just the day before. What exactly happened?

"How? When? Please tell me everything you know, everything."

"Yeah, but first you must promise to remain calm."

"I promise," Uzoma was very eager to learn of the events that got her father to the hospital.

"Well, when we got to the village yesterday, we noticed that your uncle, Ndukaku, had converted your late grandma's house into a poultry farm without the consent of your father. He even pulled down some walls to restructure the building to his desire, and all without breathing a word to your father. Your father confronted him. He and his wife rained abuses on your parents. It was during the altercation that your father fell and was rushed to the village hospital. The doctor said he'd be all

94

right, but your mom is currently making arrangements to fly him back to Lagos for proper treatment. So, you don't have to worry, he'll be all right."

Uzoma was speechless for a while, then thanked Ifeoma and hung up. She sunk on the floor and wept uncontrollably for almost an hour. She knew the implication of the simple story Ifeoma told her. Her father was the first son, the diokpara. According to tradition, the obi, which is the central compound, is passed from fathers to their first sons. Other sons ought to leave the central compound at the right time and make their homes elsewhere, mostly on their inherited plots of land outside the obi.

The obi belonged to her father who could have sent his half-brother, Ndukaku, away a long time ago but for his benevolence. Her father had allowed her uncle to live in the obi, in his stepmother's (Ndukaku's mother's) house. Customarily, no one had the right to erect or fragment any structure in the obi without the consent of the first son. Now, her uncle, Ndukaku, had undermined her father because Ndukaku knew that he would inherit the obi at the demise of his brother and his son would inherit it afterwards because her father had no son.

"When will this torment end?" Uzoma sobbed. "If only I was a boy."

Uzoma knew deep in her heart that should her father die, her uncle would not hesitate to kick her and her mother out regardless of the modern edifice her father erected for them in that compound.

"Just like Mom's uncle sent Nne away," Uzoma muttered, recalling her maternal grandmother's ordeal. It happened many years before Uzoma was born. Another aspect of an

95

unjust tradition caught up with her granny. Her maternal grandfather, Nze, was the only surviving son when his father took another wife and bore his half-brother, Obidike. Nze was a famous contractor and acquired lands and properties from his business deals. Life was swift for him, his wife had four children — two boys and two girls. He was indeed a blessed man and his ship sailed smoothly until death came calling. Nze came home from work and requested a glass of water while resting on his favorite armchair. He shut his eyes and never woke up. Uzoma remembered the pain in her mother's eyes when she told her the story. Her mom, Mmachi, who was only five years old when death stole her father away, was the one who fetched him the water he never took. Despite the years that had gone by, Mmachi never forgot that fateful day when life played its tricks on her.

Nze was building a big house, a masterpiece in their central compound, as the first son before his demise. It was supposed to be an edifice, a unique structure moulded in the wealth of his talent. It was the only one of its kind in their hometown and even in the neighboring villages. Nze invested money, time, and other resources so that his family's compound would stand out. Alas, he never lived to behold the end of the beauty he created. His wife, Uzoma's grandmother, chose to honor her husband by completing his works. She sold off some of her late husband's properties to raise money and complete the house successfully. She lived in that house with her four children and her husband's stepbrother, Obidike, whom she took in as a son. Obidike was barely ten years old when Nze died, so his widow took care of Obidike, paying his fees in school as well. And they all lived together happily for a while.

Nze had sons, but his widow could not escape the clutches of tradition. Unfortunately, Nze had died before his father. Tradition indicates that if the first son dies before his father, he loses the obi whether or not he has birthed a son. It implied that the obi would ultimately be inherited by the second son, Nze's brother. Uzoma's grandmother knew the tradition but she also knew that some families choose to live together in their central compound in love and unity. Her husband's only surviving brother, Obidike, was like a son to her and had lived with her since his childhood. So she believed their family would be one of those families bound together in love and unity. But her dreams were soon cut short.

Obidike grew into a handsome and reserved man. He never forgot that Mmachi and her siblings were only his nephews and nieces and not his siblings. He also never forgot that his elder brother, Nze, died before their father and he knew the dictates of tradition. His brother's house was still an elegant place, adorned by Nze's rare collections from the different cities he worked in, valuable pieces of art. And he desired them all. When it was time for him to take a wife, Obidike called his brother's widow, Uzoma's grandmother, and, quoting the tradition, he demanded that the widow and her children left the central compound. It was then that reality set in. Nze and his widow might have built the house, his children might have felt at home there, Mmachi had even planted a pear tree that yielded lots of fruits annually, yet it was not their home nor theirs to claim. Fortunately, Mmachi's elder brother, Arinzechukwu, quickly put together a small house in a plot of land located at a good distance away from the central compound with the funds he could gather, providing shelter for his mother and siblings. This was the house in which Uzoma's grandmother still lived.

Uzoma knew her family's situation was different. If her father dies without a will, she and her mother would not only lose the village house and compound which according to tradition they would lose eventually, but they could most likely lose all their properties in Lagos as well. With an unfeeling uncle and his wife who had made no attempt to hide their contempt and scorn for her family, she was certain her life's journey would not be smooth in the event of her father's demise. Not only would her uncle covet their properties, according to tradition her uncle would stand as her father in decisions concerning her life, especially marriage. If she loses her father, her uncle would be the one to give her out in marriage. An act that even her mother was not allowed, according to tradition, to perform. Uzoma resumed her cry again, consumed by her thoughts of impending doom, she didn't hear her phone ring nor did she pick up Stefan's call.

"Save my father, O Lord," she prayed. "Heal him and save us all."

Chapter 16

Stefan was worried sick about his girl, Uzoma, who hadn't picked up his calls for hours. If only he was home, he'd have easily checked on her. He and his friends were at the ski resort in Åre for their annual skiing trip, a tradition they developed years ago. He had invited Uzoma, but she turned down his offer, claiming that she won't survive the cold in northern Sweden. Stefan had felt she conceived unspoken thoughts that were far from her given reason. He felt Uzoma would rather be anywhere than in the company of his friends. Although she said otherwise, Stefan thought she was yet to forgive them for the dinner incident. She had since avoided any meeting with them and he hadn't compelled her either. He couldn't blame her. Stefan had suggested he remain behind with Uzoma but she nudged him to go with his friends.

"Go ahead, have a time out with the guys and catch some fun. It's only for a few days anyway, and we will talk on the phone so often that you'll hardly feel my absence," she had promised. Yet he hadn't been able to get through to her since they arrived. He was getting devastated, his fun moment was robbed, leaving him solemn, unable to participate in anything. He brooded while staring at the pictures they took in his home over Christmas in the early hours of the day just before his departure and before she went back to her place.

"What could have gone wrong?" Stefan asked, speaking

to no one in particular. Uzoma looked so happy in their pictures, like she had no care in the world, radiant and beautiful. He looked at the picture of her in his mom's apron in their kitchen baking meat pie for him and his friends to take along for their journey. She looked like she belonged there, as though the kitchen was hers. He'd felt they were finally connecting on a deeper level and nursed a feeling of foreverness. How could such bliss be disrupted in mere hours? He had worked hard to get closer to her, to crumble her walls. They hadn't had sex yet, but he felt it would happen soon. She was getting more relaxed with him and increasing the amount of flesh she allowed in his view. She had even touched him, felt him in that moment of lust on Christmas Eve before she snapped out of her reverie, and pulled away. Stefan had smiled, glad that it was only a matter of time before he had her priceless gift, her innocence, her maidenhead as she called it. Now it felt like the walls were coming up again, he felt the effect of the distance between them, contrary to her promise. He missed her, his heart ached to wonder if something had happened to her. He contemplated sending someone to seek her out, but who? And how would she feel about it? She could get upset and would view him as a stalker. Or he should just go home, take the next available flight home and check on her himself. While he wallowed in such apprehension, his muse sought him out.

"Hey, babe, sorry I missed your calls. Hope you guys arrived safely?" Uzoma uttered, trying to sound as casual as possible. Yet Stefan heard the strain in her voice, something was wrong and she was trying to hide it from him.

"Ada, what's wrong?" Stefan asked bluntly. He could be forthright sometimes, and he knew it, but this wasn't the time for him to mince words. He won't let her shut him out, not this time.

"Talk to me, Ada, what's wrong?" he pressed when his initial question was met with silence. Uzoma knew better than to lie to Stefan and she knew he wouldn't give up till he got an answer.

"My father is sick," she said. "Heart attack."

She had no intention of sharing the details about the oppression her parents faced from her extended family nor about the tradition that seemed to discriminate against gender. No, she wouldn't tell him. How could she share such details with him and not look barbaric?

"Have you eaten?" Stefan asked, lost for the appropriate words to say to her. He wanted to hold her, to assure her that everything would be all right, but he knew he couldn't make such promises. Besides, Nigeria was a third world country, one he had never been to. Who knew the extent of their healthcare? If only he could do something to help or at least alleviate the pain she was feeling.

"I'm about to eat now."

"Everything will be all right," Stefan heard himself say against his better judgment.

"If you need to talk, I'm here," he added. As soon as the call ended, Stefan searched for the next available flight home. He would leave his friends, ditch their plans and dash out to her. She needed him. He shouldn't have come on the trip or he would have been with her when she got the news. She must have been crying. He could tell from her voice. What could he do to make her feel better? At that moment, he felt ineffectual. He could only wish she was all right.

Uzoma sank to her favorite place on the floor, blaming

herself for her parents' predicament. She knew the complications surrounding her birth had deprived her mother of the opportunity to birth more children. She had heard the story from her aunt, Omasirinna, her mother's only sister, and she had felt her mother Mmachi's coldness towards her a few times when Mmachi was consumed with pain for having an only child, a daughter. Uzoma knew her mom blamed her silently for the situation and that wrenched her heart. She heard from Ifeoma that her mom had succeeded in moving her father back to Lagos. If only she would pick up her calls. Uzoma went into the bathroom and immersed herself in hot water. Her parents were suffering because of her. That Igbo saying 'ajo nwa si owerri ba nne ya afo,' the evil child that entered into the mother's womb through the wrong path, must be referring to her. Because of her, her parents were suffering. Because of her, her father could lose his life and all he toiled for through the years. Because of her, her parents became an object of ridicule in society. Because of her, her mom was wilting away. She resumed her sobbing again. Her parents had provided for her needs, loved her, and sacrificed for her. Her father had stayed with them when he could have taken another wife or birthed a son through a concubine. He had chosen to be faithful to them and now he was paying the price. Uzoma wondered about the wisdom in her father's loyalty. In the end, they could lose everything. But would she have understood if her father had behaved like Mr Onyema who lived in their estate? Or would she have felt betrayed? Her father's only crime was choosing love over traditions, was choosing to remain faithful to his Christian faith by staying married to one wife, was being an honorable man rather than a deceitful person. Could the world not see this? Could tradition not see his uprightness? Uzoma couldn't decide on the central villain in the plot of her life. Should she blame God or tradition? Or should she blame the people who in her thoughts were so myopic and morally unjust to judge a wrongful act from a right one but instead punish a good man?

There must be something she could do, there must be a way to defend her parents, to right these wrongs and turn this tide around. Whatever it was, she would find it, she would save her family.

After her bath, Uzoma decided to watch a Nigerian movie, anything to distract her body and soul from the searing anguish tearing her apart. She sat on the floor mindlessly staring at the television screen as the movie played. She had chosen the first Nigerian movie she could find on YouTube, hardly mindful of the plot or the cast. She felt weak from her lack of food and constant cries. How could she eat when her dad was lying on the hospital bed battling for his life? She needed to purge herself of self-pity and put on armor to fight, to help her family. She needed the distraction the movie should provide to achieve this, to calm her nerves and think. A good sleep might help, but she knew such luxury could only exist in her wishes at that moment. As she willed herself to concentrate on the movie, the plot finally caught her attention, reminding her of an aspect of tradition she had forgotten! How could she have forgotten something so vital? Now she knew what she must do. She would use the same tradition that oppressed her family to fight for them. She would stand up to her uncle and her kinsmen with the same tradition, and she would win at all cost!

Chapter 17

Mmachi sat beside her husband's hospital bed immersed in thoughts. Why does life sway so much? She remembered the days of her youth when her husband had proposed to her and smiled dryly. Oh, she was the envy of her peers. Her husband was one of the most eligible bachelors from the neighboring village. He was tall, slim, and handsome. He was a graduate working with the petroleum industry and drove a Mercedes Benz E320, which was one of the modern cars that existed at the time. Even her own sister had been jealous when he chose her. Mmachi felt life had poured pearls at her feet, that her life would be smooth and free from worries. She knew she would never lack nor worry about food. She chuckled as she recalled. She believed she deserved it, she had lived right and it was only fair that God rewarded her with such an outstanding man.

On the day of her traditional marriage, her uncle, Obidike, acted in her late father's stead and on behalf of her elder brother because of the age difference.

"You will have male and female children," Obidike had said when he blessed her union as custom demanded after she and her husband returned the calabash used for the palm wine carrying. To Mmachi, the blessings were mere words. Her uncle simply wanted to appear upright before the people and had no true wishes for her, otherwise, the blessing would have made a difference in her life and she would have birthed a male child. If only her father were alive, he'd have blessed her out of true love and a pure heart.

Mmachi recalled the challenges that placed her in this predicament. Barely three months after marriage, the doctor confirmed she was pregnant, and she felt the universe had placed a crown on her and the angels sang in her favor. But roses do have thorns and the sun does not remain all the time. First, she was apprehensive throughout the first trimester as she bled through the weeks, then, she attempted to follow the instructions of well-meaning people who offered unsolicited advice. It was her first pregnancy and the wealth of knowledge on the internet was unavailable at the time, at least not at her disposal.

"Don't drink anything that is too cold, it will cause pneumonia for the baby in the womb," some said. "Do not eat spicy food, your baby will have rashes! Do not gratify your appetite, your baby will become too big." Many were the 'Dos' and 'Don'ts' and Mmachi, to the best of her ability, abided by them. Yet she was not free from the travails of motherhood. When labor came, the doctor had declared that she had obstructed labor and therefore recommended a caesarean section.

"God, forbid!" her mother-in-law said.

"Sister Mmachi, whose account will you believe? God's account, or the doctor's?" Brother Silas, the then leader of the Charismatics in the church, said to her.

"This is exactly what God showed me," he gloated. "I told you, Sister, the devil is moving around like a roaring lion seeking souls to destroy, but we are more than conquerors! Glory! Did you say the prayer I asked you to say, and in the manner I recommended?"

"I did everything you asked me to do," Mmachi said barely audibly, tired from the labor contractions. The pains in her abdomen were becoming excessively unbearable.

"See, Sister Mmachi, you must not lose faith now. The bible says you'll deliver like the women of the Hebrew. That is God's account, so do not listen to the doctor, rather we must pray," Brother Silas declared and led the prayers.

Brother Silas had prophesied that the doctor would recommend surgery for Mmachi rather than normal delivery. He asked Mmachi to say some prayers and to hold a feast for children around. Mmachi had said the prayers and even fasted till twelve noon for nine days during the prayer session. She sponsored children's parties in the church, visited the orphanage, and showered gifts on children she came across from then on. She did everything and even more, so why was she going through this distress? She looked up to her husband, Amechi, who was looking devastated, conflicted between the pains his wife endured and the whispers from his mother and Brother Silas. He was also burdened with the fear that his wife could die from the caesarean section. He had heard such tales and his mother did a great job reminding him at that time as well.

"Besides, all these doctors want is just money. They make more money from the surgery than normal delivery, that's why they recommend it. Your wife is healthy, there's nothing wrong with her. All she needs to do is to grit her teeth and push out the baby rather than behaving like an over-pampered child," Amechi's mother added. For Amechi, money was not the issue. He remembered all too well the cash officer in the bank he patronized who died from 'successful surgery'. The doctors declared the surgery was successful but the man never woke up, probably out of an overdose of anesthesia, rumors claimed. God, he loved his wife and couldn't imagine a life without her. He should have flown her abroad for the delivery, but the gynecologist was highly recommended. Now it was too late for that option. When he could bear the cries of his wife no more, Amechi went to the church to pray and stayed there overnight, calling in for the situation report every few minutes. He was not a fanatic, but he believed in God and accompanied his wife to church every Sunday. He prayed earnestly as he had never prayed before and made promises to God.

At the early hours of the morning, when the elderly priest came to prepare for mass, seeing a man sprawled on the floor at the altar moved the priest to inquire about his affliction.

"My son," the priest said, "God also heals through the doctors and medicines. Remember, Jesus made a spittle on one occasion when he healed a blind man. Go now and ask the doctors to do the needful."

Amechi ran to the hospital as soon as he could and granted his consent for the surgery. His wife was already losing consciousness. He had been a fool to listen to the voices around him rather than the professional. To his dismay, the surgery lasted hours, erupting a fresh wave of anxiety within him. At some point, he was certain his wife was dead and that the doctors only dragged it on to prove their worth. He banged on the theater door to no end until he was escorted out by security.

"I shouldn't have listened to the priest," he cried.

"Where are you, God? What sin have I committed that you refuse to answer my prayers?"

After a couple of hours in the theater, the doctor beckoned to him. The surgery was successful and mother and child were saved. However, an emergency hysterectomy had been carried out and his wife's uterus removed. Such situations were documented in the consent form he signed and never bothered to read. The doctor disclosed that the obstructed labor had led to the rupture of her uterus, which also resulted in bleeding (obstetrical haemorrhage).

"It's a miracle that your wife and child survived," the doctor declared. Amechi was too glad that his wife and child survived at that time to digest the meaning or implication of the hysterectomy. Brother Silas claimed that Mmachi and the baby survived because he and his group waged against the devil all through it.

Five years after Uzoma's birth, Amechi and Mmachi traveled to America for consultation with a white doctor on their reproductive problems. They could hardly trust any Nigerian doctor any more. They needed a more authentic assessment from a white wizard.

"You see the caesarean section would have easily taken care of the obstructed labor. Obstructed labor can lead to uterine rupture. And yes, emergency hysterectomy can be employed in the case of obstetrical haemorrhage caused by uterine rupture. From what I can read from your wife's medical journal you supplied, it's a miracle that she and the child survived," the white doctor had told them, validating the prognosis of the Nigerian doctor.

At first, Mmachi had blamed her husband for her misfortune, for negligence and failure to sign the consent form early enough when the doctor recommended a caesarean section. Then she blamed herself for not taking a firm decision. And when the burden of lack of a male child weighed heavily on her, she'd blame her daughter for the complication of the obstructed labor in the first place and for not coming as a male. She had reacted in different ways at different times, sometimes shutting her husband and daughter out, especially when she faced mockery from the people in the village.

Now, as she sat at the hospital watching her husband, she had a rude awakening that life was flighty and that she could lose any of her loved ones just like she lost her father. Mmachi made a conscious decision to spend the rest of her life loving the people that mattered to her and avoiding every trifling quarrel. She realized that once again, she had shut her daughter out in her trying moment and decided to call her.

"I'm sorry, baby," she cried when Uzoma answered the call. Mmachi was not just apologizing for ignoring her daughter's calls, but for her behavior through the years.

"It's OK, Mom. All will be well, you'll see," Uzoma promised.

Chapter 18

"Help me! Hurry to the house!"

The simple message Uzoma sent Stefan with exclamation marks sent him racing to her. Nothing would stop him from leaving his workplace immediately. It was past two o'clock in the afternoon on Tuesday. He'd been with her throughout the weekend as usual and she was all right when he left her. The urgency communicated through the message gave him chills. Uzoma had never sent any emergency messages in the past. What was wrong? He contemplated dialing 112, the Swedish emergency number, then thought better of it. Uzoma could have called 112 herself if she wanted them. Whatever it was, she needed him and not others. Was it her monthly period? She usually goes through pain during her flow. Still, she wasn't one to seek help at such moments either. Besides, it was too soon from the last time she had her cycle from what he could recall. Was it her father? Has his ill health worsened? Stefan entertained different thoughts as he drove hastily towards his girlfriend's home and almost ran a red light. He paid no heed to speed limits and took speed lanes where possible. She needed him and that was all that mattered to him.

It was three weeks after Stefan had aborted his skiing trip and returned to a surprisingly hearty and gleeful girlfriend. Uzoma had received him happily, wondering what he was doing in her apartment rather than skiing with his friends.

chosen, and she knew that this delicate moment would seal her fate forever, yet she didn't chicken out. She stood on the tip of her toes and pulled Stefan's cheeks down to a kiss. She would seduce him if she must until she had her way.

Stefan was carried away by lust. How long had he waited for this day? He had even dreamt about it on different occasions but never imagined it this way. When Uzoma kissed him, everything in him melted and he was ready to give her what she wanted and how she wanted it. He lifted her and went straight to bed where he worshipped her body as gently as he could before giving in fully to his thirst. And as he claimed her, he found himself. He knew right then that his search was over. He had found the one he was looking for and would live in this sweetness forever. She was his woman and he loved her in every way he could, giving her pleasure, and receiving in full as well.

"Marry me," he blurted, collapsing beside her and she chuckled dryly. Stefan turned to face her and noticed her tears.

"What is it, Ada? Did I hurt you?"

"No, Stefan, you didn't." She blinked her eyes and wiped her tears away.

"There are four people I love most in the world," she continued. "My parents, God! I'll give my life for them. I love Ifeoma as the sibling I don't have and will do all I can for her." She took a deep breath. "And I love you, Stefan, I love you much more than I ever imagined I could."

"I love you too, Ada," Stefan replied, and Ada gave her tears free rein. She knew Stefan loved her but hearing the words from him made her weak. If he had said the words to her before Christmas or even on Christmas day but before the events that happened in her hometown, she'd have swooned from the declaration. Now, the words heaped guilt on her conscience and all she could do was cry. Stefan tried to comfort her as much as he could, pulling her into his embrace, caressing her. He wondered why she was crying if she was regretting their lovemaking.

"Ada, please stop crying. I'm sorry. I wouldn't have done this if I knew you weren't ready. I thought you wanted it."

"Stefan, my tears are for that which is different from your thoughts. I cry because I love you. I cry because of tomorrow." She linked her hands with his and, gazing directly into his eyes, she said, "but for my parents, I'd go through fire for you and to the ends of the earth with you. But they gave me life, they sacrificed everything, even the life they would have had for me. It's only fair I reciprocate. I wish things were different, I wish fate had something different for me. I wish I could say yes to your abrupt, ringless proposal." She let out a whimper. "Let's live and enjoy the days as they come. Whatever happens, I want you to know that you are the one I'd have chosen any day, and if for any reason beyond my control I hurt you, I want you to remember that my love for you is true and that I'm probably hurting more."

Before Stefan could react or respond to her dirge-like speech, she claimed his lips in a kiss, silencing him. The kiss, though lacking emotion, still ignited the fire in him. Something was definitely wrong with her and her kiss had botched his attempt to inquire into the matter. Why would such a free spirit withhold herself from soaring? Her words were like stones to his heart. Why couldn't they just be happy and live in love? Was she afraid her parents wouldn't give their consent to their union?

"I could go to Nigeria and persuade them and if they won't

permit her to live in Sweden, I could relocate to Nigeria for her sake," he thought but kept the words to himself. If only she would share her fears and worries with him, if only she would let him in, he could voice his thoughts to her and they could find a solution together. He was ready to fight for their love, only if she would let him or fight with him.

Chapter 19

Uzoma decided to love as hard as she could while the opportunity remained. She knew what she had done and that soon happiness would elude her. She knew karma was a dreadful witch and nature would judge her, yet she couldn't undo what she had done for her parents' sake. She stared at the pregnancy test strip in her hands. It read in Swedish: pregnant, three weeks+. She ought to be happy. Her hard work paid off. She got what she wanted, yet she found herself sad and mournful. Her insides churned. If only she could share the news with Stefan. No, she would make sure he was ignorant of this. She had betrayed him in the worst possible way. She knew he wanted no child yet she got herself knocked up by him. She couldn't imagine what he'd say or do if he found out she was carrying his child and much less if he discovered what she had done to lure him into her ploy. Could her motive justify her dubious ways? Her guilt weighed heavily on her conscience. The drugs she fed Stefan were fertility drugs she turned into a multivitamin case. She did the same for hers. How deceptive can one be? She had appraised herself as a God-loving steadfast Christian who tried to live as upright as possible. Now she felt darker than sin. She knew her actions were evil and wicked. She had betrayed his trust. She knew he slept with her that day without protection because he trusted her and believed her words.

"But I didn't tell him I was free, I didn't say I won't get pregnant. I only told him it was OK." Uzoma tried to find solace in the choice of words she used when she lured Stefan. Although her words didn't expressly indicate she was in her free period, she knew the words implied it.

Though in reality, she meant that she had meticulously calculated her ovulation day. She had used an ovulation test kit and that fateful afternoon, she felt mild ovulation pain, confirming her hypothesis. She had sent him the emergency text to hasten his arrival. She wanted him to perform the act while the pain persists. So she had deceived Stefan through and through. She wanted to cry, to weep for her sins, for her cruelty against the one she loved. But even her own tears had deserted her. What right did she have to claim love? Love was not wicked, no. Deep in her heart, she knew she cared about him so much, but she had allowed the beast in her to eat up her love. She had sold her true love for the sake of her parents, to explore the other side of tradition, to triumph against her greedy and covetous uncle. But did that justify her actions? What about Stefan? What about his feelings, his love, his trust? What he doesn't know won't kill him, she thought.

Should she break off their relationship? It would spare him further manipulation. Also, if she kept him closer, he could discover her secrets. Her heart broke. How would she live in Sweden and within the same city as Stefan and ignore him? If only she was through with her thesis, she could have simply returned to Nigeria. Thankfully, she was in her final semester. She made up her mind to leave the country before her pregnancy became palpable.

Uzoma decided to discard the test strip, doing so in the waste bin outside the building. Then, she replaced Stefan's fertility drugs with multivitamin tablets and hers with Pregnacare. She would call off the relationship at the right time. But when would that be? She abhorred her actions and as she looked into the mirror in the bathroom, she felt she reeked of evil, betrayal, and shame.

Downcast, she picked up her phone and sent Stefan a message.

"I'm so sorry, querida," she wrote.

"What for?" His reply brought her back to reality. What had she done? She had given in to grief when she sent that message. She tarried, and as she wondered what to reply, Stefan called.

"Hi, babe. Are you ok? What are you sorry for?"

"I'm fine. I just feel I haven't treated you as good as I ought to and I'm sorry about it. I feel I don't deserve you, Stefan." She was being honest without revealing the facts. It broke her to withhold so many secrets from him. He was indeed a good man and she truly did not deserve him. Her eyes finally moistened and she gladly gave in to tears.

"Hey, are you crying?" Stefan asked, confused. "Ada, you've treated me just fine. I do not know a better way you could have shown your love. You even gave me your rare gift, your virginity."

Uzoma began to weep more when she heard that. If only Stefan knew the motive behind her gift. Not that she wouldn't have given it to him eventually, she almost did on Christmas Eve, but her quest had thwarted the sacredness and the purity of her gift. She wept so hard that she was unaware that Stefan had ended the call, nor was she aware of the moments that had passed until she saw Stefan standing before her.

"Ada, please stop crying," he said and lifted her off of the toilet seat where she had been sitting all through it.

"I know you hold back sometimes," Stefan continued, "but besides that, you've cared for me as much as I do you. I love you just the way you are and wish we can spend the rest of our lives together. Stop crying, babe. You're perfect for me. I am willing to relocate to Nigeria if it would make you happy, as long as we are together."

"No, Stefan. I won't allow you to make more sacrifices for me. I do not deserve it," Uzoma said between sobs.

"Shh, you deserve it and even more," Stefan insisted and claimed her lips with his while she gave in to pleasure, tucking her pain away as they made love — protected like they've done a number of times after the first.

Stefan wondered if he should get a vasectomy. He wanted Uzoma to himself without the intrusion of any baby. But he knew she wanted babies. She had told him that much. This was one thing they do not share the same thoughts on. If he got a vasectomy, would she leave him? What if he gave in to her wishes and gave her a child? He knew it would make her happy and he loved her enough to do anything for her. He had seen her with kids, she'd make a great Mom, only her attention would be divided, and she'd probably love him less. No one can serve two masters at a time. She would either love him more and neglect the child like his parents or she would love the child more and neglect him. The latter stung his heart. No, he won't allow a child to come between them. And if he failed to resolve this difference, would it cost him his relationship? Why was life so complicated? If only he was enough for her, he'd give her the world.

Stefan admired Uzoma as she slept peacefully beside him. He loved her so much. If only he could take all her pains away.

He decided against the vasectomy. If Uzoma would accept his proposal, maybe sometime in the future, in the farthest future, he might give her what she wanted. He explored the thought further. If she would settle with him, they could spend the first ten years of their lives together living for themselves. After all, they were still in their mid-twenties. They could consider the option of a baby afterwards, maybe in their mid-thirties. The plan sounded solid to Stefan, he would let her in on it when she accepts his proposal. He smiled and, giving in to fatigue, dozed off beside his desired companion.

Chapter 20

Amechi sat on the balcony upstairs, longing for some alone time. It's been two days since he returned from the hospital and their home has been buzzing with well-meaning people, church members, neighbors and work colleagues offering their good wishes. He knew the wishes were not all representative of their true feelings towards him. The rumor of his ill health had spread. Some visited merely to confirm the state of his health. The hawks were gathering, he could feel them. He knew such deep thoughts made his blood pressure rise and could constrict his blood vessels further. Although the surgery performed on him was to open up the blocked vessels, the doctor had warned of the possible dangers ahead and the risk of recurrence.

"With good food and proper exercise, you should be fine," the doctor had told him.

Really, would he be fine? And for how long before another attack which could claim his life comes calling? One year? Two? Amechi felt like the end was near. God, what if he hadn't survived this one? He wasn't prepared, he was yet to organize his 'house.' At that moment, Amaechi wished he had a son. A son that would inherit his company and run his business, a son that could ward off the hawks. He knew it was only a matter of time before his partners and competitors tore up his life's sweat, everything he had worked for.

A few years after his marriage to Mmachi, he left the oil company to set up a business. After all, he was an Igbo man, and they were known for their business prowess. Like many others from his tribe, he had gone into importation, importing and supplying building materials such as tiles, security doors, bathroom accessories, and finishings, then expanded into furniture as well. His wife encouraged and supported him all through it. They made every decision together and his business soared. But despite her contributions behind the scene, she had never been an active part of his company. She hardly came to the office or looked at the account, neither did she know the details of the products they supplied nor their clients aside from those he had hosted in their home.

Amechi wondered how his family would cope in his absence. He loved his daughter so much and wished that her life would continue on a smooth plane. Who would protect his beloved daughter and ensure that she never lacked? Who would protect her from the harsh realities of life? His heart bled. If only she was a boy, the game would have been different and so many hawks would not be hovering around. Had he made the wrong decision? Was it wrong of him to have chosen the love of his family over polygamy? He wanted to save his family from the hostility he experienced growing up in a polygamous home. If he and his stepbrother, Ndukaku, were of the same mother, would Ndukaku spite him this much? Amaechi loved his brother but Ndukaku had only seen him as a rival and even an enemy, arrogantly exuding his hatred and preying on his weakness. What if he had listened to his mother? What if he had kept a baby mama? Sure, it would have broken Mmachi, his dear wife, but his assets could be saved. And what if this other woman and her sons coveted all and scorned his beloved wife and daughter? No, he'd rather not have that. What other choice did he have? If he had adopted a male child, like his wife suggested, what is the guarantee that this child would possess the qualities he wanted in a son and carry on his legacy? That would be giving the mantle to a stranger to decide the fate of his family. Either way, he felt doomed and his worry at the moment would bear no fruits nor would it ward off the storm.

"Please avoid anything stressful that could increase your blood pressure. We don't want your pipes blocking again, to avoid another heart attack," the doctor had cautioned Amechi before he left the hospital.

Easier said. Amechi knew his biggest challenge. He could easily abide by the recommended diets and exercises, but the social issues that plagued him and the zeal to keep his business afloat could jeopardize his health. He was distressed from brooding on the aftermath of his life and on the choices he had made in the past.

"Everything would be all right, Dad, I promise. Just believe me and trust God," his beloved daughter promised. Amechi allowed himself a wry smile, his precious little girl was trying to assuage his feelings. His innocent and simple-minded child. If only life was so simple. Amechi wished he could shield her from the harsh storms of life to preserve her innocence and to maintain her panorama of the world's beauty. He ought to pen down his testament, he knew it was the right thing to do. God had given him a second chance to organize his family. Besides, he wouldn't put it past his brother to claim his properties, especially in the absence of a will, and tradition would back him as would some of his kinsmen who would want their share.

It broke his heart as he wondered. He had been good to his kin, bearing gifts of food items and money which he distributed every festive season. Yet, he knew only a few of them were grateful, some were envious, and others felt entitled. How many young men among his kin had he rendered assistance to establish a business? How many had returned to thank him and how many had returned to ask for more? Amechi recalled the young man, Obinna, whom he turned away after he had assisted the young man twice. He recalled the statement Obinna's father made when Amechi maintained his resolve not to give Obinna any more money despite the father's plea. "You think you're God because you have money? I stand here begging you as a brother but you act like the world is at your feet. We shall see!" he threatened before storming out of Amaechi's presence. Amaechi knew Obinna's father would easily hop on the same boat with Ndukaku and assail his family.

How could they feel so entitled? Amechi could hardly recall any of his uncles or relatives offering him a dime in the past, even as a lad, yet they all felt entitled to his wealth. Would the king step in to help his family if he was no more? Amechi had donated large sums for different projects in his village. He had even granted scholarships to some wards in the community. Even his nephews and nieces benefited from this, yet his brother spat at him so. How could he be certain of the true feelings of others?

Onye n'eme eme k'ana afuru oru — faults are found in a helper. Amechi mulled over the adage. How true. People easily summarize the tight-fisted and pay them no heed, but the kind-hearted were often dissected and their actions, x-rayed for faults. He knew he couldn't please everyone, even Jesus didn't. Amechi only hoped his good deeds were enough to yield long-lasting fruits in the life of his daughter.

In the meantime, Amechi resolved to pen his testament and scout for loyal people among his staff whom he could elevate and entrust the operations of his business. He wanted his daughter to live her life according to her own inclinations. As was his wont, Amechi had not imposed anything on Uzoma. No. He would rather she lived her dreams than compel her to run his business. If Amechi had a son, would he have been so liberal with the son?

Chapter 21

Uzoma peered outside the window on the plane, lost in thoughts. She hadn't eaten anything since the morning. She couldn't get anything down her throat. It was bad for her condition and she knew it, but the pain she felt ripped her insides.

Would she ever see Stefan again?

She could still feel the warmth of his lips when he kissed her goodbye at the airport, his eyes filled with unshed tears.

"Call me as soon as you arrive, Ada," Stefan instructed.

Uzoma decided she would call him to ease his worry, but she had no intentions of keeping her other promises to him. She had promised to return and had packed a little bag to buttress her point. She knew Stefan would have insisted on traveling with her if she had divulged her true intentions. Thankfully, he needed a visa to go to Nigeria and she deliberately informed him of her journey at the last minute to thwart him from attempting to accompany her.

It was three months after Uzoma confirmed her pregnancy. She had worked tirelessly to complete her thesis and submit it before the pregnancy bump revealed her condition. Stefan noticed the changes in her body — her increased body weight, enlarged breasts, her voracious appetite, and glowing skin. Uzoma had blamed her appetite on multivitamins, her body weight and full breasts on the excess food intake. She had promised him a good time at the gym after her thesis to quell his concerns. Uzoma mulled at how easily she could deceive Stefan. She knew he wasn't a goon. He was only too trusting and open-minded to harbor suspicions. Yet, she knew it was only a matter of time before he happened on the truth, a risk she was unwilling to take.

The academic work provided a perfect distraction and a justifiable reason to put a safe distance between herself and her lover. Although Stefan continued the ritual of spending his weekends with her, Uzoma ensured those days were filled with tasks such that she had little time to spare. Thankfully, she experienced nothing like the morning sickness she read about online, or Stefan might have forced her to go to the hospital. Stefan remained steadfast, loving her from the distance she created without complaints, silently lending his support with a promise of a wonderful summer vacation at the end of her studies.

"We can go to Asia, South Korea. I've been longing to visit Seoul and Jeju Island." Uzoma fueled his fantasies in one of the rare moments she allowed herself a break to embrace him. Her push-and-pull mechanism was her only way of saving him from the heartache an outright breakup would bring, or maybe she was simply selfish, protecting her secrets while enjoying his care. Either way, her final moments in Sweden were bitter-sweet as she couldn't totally tuck away the future to enjoy the present and she would cry when overwhelmed with feelings of love and regret. But the deed was done and there was no going back.

"Whatever you want, my love," Stefan acquiesced, occupied in thoughts, wondering if the trip could really rebuild their relationship. He knew something was amiss. Uzoma would snap over little things, foam on the bathroom wall after taking his bath or an unarranged shoe. She even complained over a smelling poop and was easily taken to tears. The mood swings were so apparent that he walked on eggshells and was tempted to stay away. How could he when she was also quick with apologies? Stefan pegged it on her father's ill-health and the pressures from school. The few moments they spent planning for the future, the nearest future, the summer holiday, kept him hopeful. All before the news of her sudden trip to Nigeria.

"What do you consider the worst thing, an unforgivable sin, that I can commit against you?" Uzoma queried Stefan one bright Saturday afternoon, a few days before her departure. Stefan was stunned into silence, completely taken aback by the question. He couldn't conceive of a sin he wouldn't forgive. He would be hurt if she cheated on him, but he could forgive her if she were truly repentant.

"I'd rather focus on the things you could do to make me happy," Stefan answered, refusing to dwell on negativity, lest she tempt him by carrying out any act he might voice.

"And what would they be?" She winked at him.

"I wish you would be your usual self, the fun and jovial girl I fell in love with. You've suddenly become… a little cantankerous, crying over the slightest provocation. I know you're traumatized by the events at home, but I wish we could be as we were before now." Stefan took her hands in his and, staring deep into her eyes, added, "I miss us. I miss you. I miss the woman you were."

"What if the girl you knew was long gone?" Uzoma replied, abashed. She walked away from him over to her desk and penned the words that burned in her heart:

"Would you still love me if the structure you see were only but shadows?

Would you still love me when the sun fades, and the sky threatens a downpour?

Would you still love me when my imperfections are brought to fore and the glory you see glooms?

Would you still love me when fumes of our colors pollute the air around us and rules made by men cage our very soul?

Would you still love me when that which you now hold becomes a vapor you can hardly see?

Would you still love when I stand not as one but two?"

The words she etched on the paper bore in-depth the truth she failed to tell. If only she knew the answer. If only love could truly surmount the barriers that yet stands between them. A barrier of love challenged by love, honor, and filial duty; a barrier caused by the laws of men, men who delight themselves as lords over significant others and, fanning their ego, subjugating those whom they deem weak.

Uzoma folded the paper then handed it over to Stefan, her expression unreadable. As she expected, she got no reply from Stefan. She knew her words were riddles he could hardly fathom, not without the knowledge of things she had hidden from him.

"I want to travel to Nigeria to see my father," she declared.

"Oh really? When would you like to go? I can come…"

"No need," Uzoma interrupted. "I'll go alone."

Stefan's eyes revealed the hurt he felt at Uzoma's quick dismissal.

"I feel I must visit soon, my love," she coerced. "I fear

that if I tarry while you get a visa, I might not meet my father alive. I'll return sooner than you imagine."

"And you can join me if I don't return as planned," Uzoma quickly added when she noticed that Stefan was about to protest and sealed her quest. She knew she had no plans of returning to Sweden and ought to create memories she could harbor for years to come in her last moments with her heartthrob, yet she spent those days mourning the tear she initiated, the shredding of a love so pure.

Now, as she peered through the window of the airplane, her heart jolted as the plane touched the tarmac. She was home. Uzoma's legs quivered as she stepped off of the plane. No one was waiting for her. She had kept her journey a secret for no specific reason. She'd rather break the news of her "illegitimate baby" to her parents in person than have them sift the truth from her on the phone. They could suspect that something was amiss if she informed them of her early return. Or maybe her hurting heart would rather not deal with extra drama before it became absolutely necessary.

Rolling her hand luggage, she hailed a taxi. The scene was an irony to the day she departed the country for Sweden when she had her parents and Ifeoma with her at the airport. She had taken three large suitcases with her when she left for Sweden. Now, she returned with only hand luggage and a broken and heavy heart. Oh, and a seed of love growing within her, the symbol of her love for her parents and her great betrayal of love.

Suddenly, she felt guilty, dirty, and unworthy. What would her parents say? What judgment would posterity bring her way? And what would be the outcome of the choices she had made? She needed someone to talk to. She had harbored her secret alone, divulging nothing to no one, not even her closest friend and sister, Ifeoma.

"Please stop by the catholic church on Toyin street," Uzoma instructed the cab driver as the need to bear her soul consumed her.

She walked into the empty church, fell to her knees and wailed. Her lips could form no words. She was a sinner. She had sinned against man and God, and against love, shattering the rare gift she got. How could she begin to seek forgiveness when even the bible abhors extramarital sex? She couldn't even recall the last day she stepped foot in any church hall. She felt unworthy, so unworthy to seek the Lord's help. Uzoma wet the floor around her with her tears and felt lighter. She would face tomorrow with her shoulders high and accept the thorns that would come with the path she had chosen. She braced herself, picked up her luggage, and stepped into her course.

Chapter 22

"You're awake, Ada, thank God!" Mmachi exclaimed as she sat by her daughter's hospital bedside. It had been four hours since the surgery ended and she had been worried sick about Uzoma's state of unconsciousness, fretting, praying, pacing and complaining. No one could get her to relax. Mmachi couldn't imagine losing her only child, it would be the worst fate to befall her as a mother. She tarried by her daughter's hospital bedside watching over her every second, neither eating nor drinking. At that moment, all she wanted was to see her daughter live. Her initial worry, when the doctor declared the surgery a necessity, had worn out. At first, Mmachi was dispirited that her daughter could be saddled with the same fate she had, but as she watched Uzoma lying there on the hospital bed looking bleak, she could only ask for life.

"Mom," Uzoma called barely audibly. "Dad," she acknowledged as her father hurried to her bedside. A feeble smile was all she could offer. Her stomach hurt from the site of the surgery.

"You made it, my princess. I'm so proud of you," Amechi planted a kiss on his daughter's forehead. He had been greatly perturbed also, but for his wife's sake, he had taken a semblance that concealed the reality. That was his only bait to unnerve the anxiety that almost drove him into punching walls. He'd have never forgiven himself if he had lost his daughter to the tumultuous storm life threw his way. He felt like a coward who allowed a little child to save him from drowning. As a father, he wished his daughter didn't sacrifice her life, her youth, for his sake. But as a man, an Igbo man, he was glad he finally had someone to present to his kin and deplete his brother's ego. Unabashed, he beamed in the lustre of his victory.

"Where is my son?" Uzoma asked. Mmachi picked up the tiny tot and brought him to behold his mother's face.

"Daddy, have you given him a name yet?"

"He shall be called Onochie, for he is to replace me when I join my ancestors," Amechi replied.

"Very well, Dad, his name is Onochie and his middle name Stefansson." Uzoma wanted her son to have something of his birth father, and according to the age-long Swedish practice, decided to call her son Stefansson, which implies Stefan's son. Stabbed by guilt at the implication of the middle name she had given her son, she glanced at her father who tried in vain to hide a gust of sadness. Uzoma knew the reason for her father's crestfallen countenance. Amechi had only moments ago pronounced the new baby Onochie and basked in the delight of having a son. The name Stefansson would only serve as a reminder that he truly was not the baby's biological father, despite tradition.

"All will be well," Mmachi coerced as she caressed her daughter's arm, perceiving her discomfort.

"My grandson is so cute."

Uzoma wiped the tear that escaped her eyes. Indeed, her son was cute in his light skin and blue eyes. The very traits that reminded her of his birth father. It's been five months since she left Sweden, five months of fruitless attempt to forget Stefan, five months of surviving rather than living. For a moment, she almost wished she died in the theater so she could escape the torture and her parents could raise her child as fully theirs. She could see the delight on their faces as they watched the little one.

"Life," she thought. Only months ago, her mother had been disappointed when she returned home pregnant.

"How could you do this to us? After all the sacrifices we made for you? How could you bring shame to the family? Our enemies would laugh at us. We sent you to Sweden to get a certificate and not to prostitute yourself and return with an unwanted pregnancy," her mother had said.

"To say I'm disappointed is an understatement," her father had added.

Uzoma had choked with tears as she listened to her parents' condemnation.

"What will people say?" her mother continued. "And I'm the leader of the Catholic Women's Organization at church. My enemies have gotten me. I might even be prevented from receiving communion."

Uzoma had offered no explanations. She pushed herself upstairs and locked herself in her room till the next day and her parents were too disappointed to care. That night, Uzoma considered suicide. The very people she chose over her happiness had turned their backs on her. They had given her no room to offer explanations. She contemplated returning to Sweden, but the horror of Stefan's possible reaction doused her desire. She'd rather he remembered her as a saint than as a villain who deceived him. Besides, if she stayed back in Nigeria, she would have Ifeoma at least, to lean on. In Sweden, she'll be all alone if Stefan turned from her. She opted to remain in Nigeria, to carry her cross and to live for her child. The innocent baby deserved a chance at life.

Days after her return, Mmachi begrudgingly took Uzoma to the hospital to register for antenatal. Only when the scan revealed the sex of the baby did her mother's demeanor towards her change. Although Mmachi would have preferred that her daughter didn't get herself knocked up, she was glad Uzoma was carrying a male child.

Uzoma spent weeks speaking to none of her parents, keeping to herself and only eating as little as she could to stay alive. Her father made it easier on her by avoiding her also as much as he could until his health deteriorated and he became hospitalized again. Uzoma had wept bitterly. Her decision to bear her parents a son could cost her father's life.

"Daddy, please don't leave me. Stay with me, Daddy. I'm so sorry." It was the first time Uzoma apologized for her decision.

"Daddy, I only wanted to give you a son. Tradition indicates that the child of an unmarried woman belongs to her father. Daddy, tradition permits me to stay unmarried and raise a son or sons for my father. Daddy, all I wanted was to give you the son my birth robbed you of. All I wanted was to make you stand tall among your kinsmen. All I wanted was a son to inherit the works of your labor. All I wanted was to give you a reason to live longer and not a reason to leave me," she wept.

Amaechi hugged his daughter in tears.

"I knew I didn't raise a loose child. You shouldn't have sacrificed your life, your youth, for me, Ada," he cried. That moment returned peace to their home and Uzoma got all the support she needed from her family. Her father sold their house and bought a new one on the island where no one knew them, so she could move around freely and not be taunted by people in the estate. Amechi knew that society would frown at her daughter's illegitimate pregnancy and tongues would wag irrespective of their abode, but he'd rather they faced judgement from unknown people than the mockery of friends. If only he could turn back the hands of time, if only he knew his daughter's intentions, he'd have dissuaded her from it and saved her from a lifetime of ridicule.

"If only she knows that people will always refer to this incident," Amechi thought to himself. He resolved to be a pillar for his family, for his daughter. And at the right time, he could discourage her from remaining single and to get married if the opportunity presents itself.

Amechi, Mmachi, and Ifeoma doted on Uzoma all through the remaining weeks of her pregnancy. She was already in her thirty-seventh week when her swollen feet and constant headache led her to seek healthcare and she was diagnosed with pre-eclampsia. When the doctor recommended a caesarean section partly because of her condition but mostly due to the shape of her pelvic bone, buried demons resurfaced to taunt the family. This time, Amaechi consented to the prescribed course of action, though he drowned in fear. Like his wife, Mmachi, he stood close to the theater, interceding in prayers within him. Despite the counsel and reassurances, the white doctor he visited years ago in America with Mmachi had given them that CS was nothing bad, he could not help the anxiety that engulfed him. Now in his daughter's hospital room, he voiced his gratitude to God for the life of his daughter and that of his son, his grandson.

Uzoma was not ungrateful for the gift of life, and although she couldn't cuddle her son yet, she loved him fiercely. Her sullen feeling was borne out of the thoughts of Stefan that occupied her mind. Her son reminded her of her squelched relationship and her embittered heart. Tired, she watched as her parents tried to cajole a smile from Onochie. She smiled, hopeful for tomorrow and drifted into a restful slumber.

Chapter 23

Uzoma walked back to the salon in the estate. She had forgotten her phone there when she went to braid her hair. As was her wont when she wasn't leaving the estate, she walked rather than drove.

"Yes, she's the one. I heard her parents sent her abroad to study and she went there to do ashawo and only returned when she got pregnant," Uzoma overheard one of the stylists say. She stopped in her tracks and listened to the gossip.[6]

"Such an ungrateful girl. What does she lack? Her parents are rich. I see her all the time cruising in different cars, yet she can't keep her legs closed," another chipped.

"Her son attends the same school as my children. She's always puffed up as though everyone is beneath her. Which one is her name, Uzoma or Ada? I hear people call her the two," a customer said.

"Uzoma, my sister. It's so funny that these rich spoilt children have no shame. If I were in her shoes, I'd bend my head in shame. After one acting like a queen. Which man would want to marry such an akwuna."[7]

"And did anyone tell you she has any intentions of getting married?" Uzoma asked as she entered the salon. She had heard enough. It wasn't the first time she heard people make

---

[6] prostitution
[7] prostitute

remarks on her character or refer to her as a prostitute. Yet she felt hurt. Only a few minutes ago they were laughing heartily with her like a friend, only to judge and condemn her behind her back. How exactly did she wrong them or carry herself pompously? She always chatted heartily with them each time she visited the salon and gave them substantial tips.

"Next time you want to tell my story, tell it properly. The country is Sweden and I finished my studies. If your definition of an ashawo is a woman who fell in love with a man, then I'm guilty." Uzoma smiled wryly, picked up her phone and left the salon.

As she walked home, Uzoma wondered at her life and at the choices she made. It's been three years since Onochie was born. Three years since people berated her. The stigma seemed to follow her everywhere she went. Her father's purpose for relocating them to a new environment appeared futile. People could easily tell that Onochie was too young to be her parents' biological child, and from his skin color they could easily surmise that his father was white. It was really not rocket science to link it all to her and it appeared as though people would rather ride on their assumptions, especially when it paints another as a monster, than seek the truth. If only she could show the world that her son was indeed a product of love. If only she could reveal her true feelings for the father of her child. She hadn't contacted Stefan except for the safe arrival message she sent to him the day she got back. She had deleted her WhatsApp and all her social media handles and created new ones. She couldn't tell him the truth and couldn't break up with him properly either. She was a coward and she knew it. She knew her disappearance would devastate him, and she hoped he'd move on. At least that was what she told herself to assuage her guilt when in reality, she wished she could have him back and live happily ever after together. But if he moved on, at least he wouldn't remember her as the lady who betrayed him but as one who disappeared.

Now she wondered, did she make the right decision? Her parents were happy and doted on Onochie. His wishes were their command. Her father even threw an elaborate party in the village to introduce Onochie to his kinsmen as the son to carry on his lineage. Uzoma chuckled. How many times had she heard people in the village refer to her child as nwa onye ocha — a white man's child? Will they ever truly accept Onochie as one of them? His light skin (though tanned), curly hair, and his blue eyes would always give him away. They would always see his color first.

Yes, her father has got an heir and his properties, especially the Obi, might have been saved. But would Onochie be able to stand amongst the kinsmen? Would anyone ever regard him as the son of the clan, or would people jest that he was born of a foreign father and was, therefore, a foreigner? After all, Nigeria was a patriarchal society and children belonged to their fathers and are natives of their fathers' hometowns, not their mothers'. Would Onochie be able to live in her father's shadow and accept ridicule all his life?

Onochie was beginning to ask questions in subtle and indirect ways. The lad was too smart for his age. Although he called Amaechi, his grandfather, 'Daddy', Mmachi, his grandmother, 'Mommy', and Uzoma, his mother, 'Ada', he only did so because every other person at home called the trio these names. The little one had complained that people in school called him Oyibo (white) and wondered why. Uzoma could perceive that he knew her parents were not his biological parents, and he looked a bit different from the rest of the family. Soon he would know the reality and although he had many friends in school, children who wished to be friends with him because he was different, he could be affected psychologically if everyone continued to refer to his difference.

Uzoma thought of a solution. She could transfer him to another school. Maybe the British International School where he'd be in the midst of other white children. If only she could shield him from the damning statements of the ignorant lots. If only she could protect him from hearing tales that he was the product of his mother's loose character. If only she could guard him from the taunt of people among whom he should belong, then she would have peace and her life could become a little savory. One day he would ask about his father, or the reason he was the only very light skinned and blue-eyed member of the family, what would her reply be? When Onochie learns the truth surrounding his birth, would he be docile enough to accept his identity and position as Amechi's heir or would he rather seek to return to his biological father? According to tradition, he was Amechi's son and heir and would remain so, but would he be interested in taking up traditional responsibilities as Amechi's heir in the future especially when Amechi had gone to join his ancestors? As the first son or only son of the family, Onochie would be required to take vital decisions on behalf of the family and attend kindred meetings in the absence of Amechi. He would also be required to have children that would carry on the family's name and ensure that Amechi's linage continued. Would Onochie when he becomes an adult declare like his father Stefan that he would prefer not to father any child? The environment should have an influence on him concerning this. If he remained in Nigeria, he would most likely view procreation as a duty and not an option. But if Onochie returned to Sweden where he could develop an individualistic mindset and decides not to have children, then it could be the end of Amechi's linage.

Maybe Uzoma had been too myopic and didn't think about the future. She hadn't factored the impact of her decision on the child who obviously would bear the brunt. Not that she was spared from the malicious attacks of people, but her major concern as a mother at the moment was her child.

For three years, she had neither liked nor dated any man. She had embedded herself in her work managing her father's company, and despite Amaechi's initial resistance because of her sex, she was great at her job. She began going to her father's office with her father six months after Onochie's birth. Almost the same length of time it took her to convince the father to allow her work as his assistant.

"I need a job, Father, I can't stay at home forever doing nothing and I'd rather work for you than for someone else. Besides, it's high time another member of the family got involved in the family business. Who knows what tomorrow holds?" Uzoma pushed. Gradually she learned the nitty gritty of the establishment and had since grown competent enough to act in her father's stead. Her reason for taking this step was to ensure that the company would not be left in the hands of strangers in case of any eventualities. At first the job was merely a duty to Uzoma but it soon became her escape zone. When the weight of her past decisions and failed relationship closed in on her, Uzoma escaped depressive feelings by working harder. She came up with proposals to expand the business into other states in Nigeria and travelled often to those states to oversee the expansions. Uzoma knew Onochie had enough people doting on him especially her mother Mmachi. She knew he was well taken care of and so she confidently went about her duties without worries. She loved her son so much but he also served as a reminder of what she lost. Uzoma spent time with Onochie when she could and took him to school herself when her schedule permitted. Other times she kept herself so busy and away from him. Her parents ensured she was part of any decision making concerning Onochie and that guaranteed she acted in some small capacity, as the birth mother of the lad. She printed the pictures she took with Stefan while in Sweden and kept in a safe alongside the hard disk in which she saved the soft copies. It enabled her get rid of the pictures from her phone and laptop so she wouldn't brood over them and at the same time, it enabled her to preserve them for her son. She hoped that when the time of reckoning came, the moments captured in the pictures would reveal her bond with Stefan to Onochie and convince him that he wasn't just a product of manipulation but of love.

Uzoma knew having a child out of wedlock was a turnoff for men, especially those from her tribe. Not that she had any intentions to date any man, but sometimes she wished she had someone to hold or cuddle her to sleep, someone to share her bed, someone to call her own. For how long would she remain single and celibate? Would she ever date again or even get married? Or would she live the rest of her life as a maiden in her father's house? Would she be able to find love again? She missed Stefan. She missed their time together and sometimes she was tempted to reach out to him, to send an email or a letter to his parents' home or to seek him out on social media. But would Stefan want to hear from her? Sometimes she felt he deserved to know about Onochie. How would he feel if he discovered he had a son? He would be shattered. He never wanted a child. The news of having one would sadden him.

"Stefan deserves to be happy. I'd better let sleeping dogs lie," Uzoma decided. Although she knew not what lay ahead and she might never find love again, she would live her life loving her son and hope that her secret remained buried. But is there anything permanently hidden under the sun?

Lightning Source UK Ltd.
Milton Keynes UK
UKHW010944140722
405852UK00001B/164